MW01100340

Playing for Pancho Villa

"Sterling Bennett has lived in Mexico long enough and has listened to the rhythms of Mexican life closely enough to capture the pulse and the color of old Mexico in his new novel *Playing for Pancho Villa*.

"Weaving historical figures and fictional characters into a bittersweet tale of love and adventure, Bennett has created an epic that can be read and appreciated by Americans of any nationality, whichever side of the border where they happen to live and work.

"*Playing for Pancho Villa* makes a perfect gift for...any holiday or celebration. Villa himself might want it...."

—Jonah Raskin, author of *My Search for B. Traven,*
Professor Emeritus, Sonoma State University, California

PLAYING FOR PANCHO VILLA

STERLING BENNETT

DEDICATION

For Dianne

NOTEBOOKS AND NIBBLES

For years I have hesitated to approach this story. What I know about my grandfather Frank comes from the lips of scoffing aunts, my grandmother—from whom I am said to have my soft brown eyes—and a discovered steamer trunk where a rat or two had eaten away a hole in the front and settled down inside, nibbling on an impressive mound of letters, journals and abandoned manuscripts, decorating them with droppings . . . and a pungent comment here and there. I don't mention the rats in order to give legitimacy, but simply to point out that they were better acquainted with my grandfather's writing than I was. Of course, as a child I had watched him scribble his pages.

He preferred the same six-by-eight notebooks I used in grades three through five, and he bent over and whispered when he wrote, as if telling a story to someone he knew or had once known . . . to the extent that I sometimes glanced sideways at the darker parts of the room to be sure no one else was there. At times, his words got stuck on an "s" and became no more than a gently pulsing hiss.

Later, he told me strange stories, bits and pieces about horses and guns, all of which interested no one in the family, and only made me want to have a gun of my own so I could shoot small animals and pretend to be a soldier.

Later still, when he could only move his lips but not say anything, I could tell from the way he looked at me that he still had more he wanted to say but couldn't, because—from age and the sickness that had always been with him—his hands shook too much to write. And then he died and I didn't really think about him too much until the trunk was discovered.

My big sister—who had bought out the rest of us—decided the time had come to change the old barn into an urban dwelling with Jacuzzi. With her own powerful arms, she pried open a long-forgotten, boarded-up closet—making the eight penny nails screech—and forever ended the peace of the trunk's current occupants.

The contents of the trunk were largely un-nibbled, perhaps out of respect . . . or fear of words. Or, like my family, from an abiding disinterest. A disorder reigned, perhaps from long winter nights with nothing for whiskered noses to do but push around notebooks, or—before that—from my grandfather returning often to touch the memories of his life.

I talked to family members, the aunts—my uncles were already dead—my mother and father, who, because they were New Englanders—or maybe because they were hiding some embarrassment—guarded his privacy with impenetrable looks and long hesitations.

Now more years have passed, and I have at last decided, while there is still time, to give a human order to the trunk's contents. As much to know who I am myself as to tell his story of deserts, guns, horses and love.

—Liam Holloway
Tucson, Arizona
March 23, 2012

CHAPTER 1

Guns and Goats

¿A dónde vas, conejo Blas,
con esa escopeta
colgada detrás?
Where you going, Rabbit Blas,
with that rifle
hanging on your back?

—The children's song by Cri-Crí.

In 1916, my grandfather, Frank Holloway, at the age of twenty-eight, got mercury poisoning working in the Silver Creek Mine in Mogollón, New Mexico. His doctor told him to have an adventure and get away from the mine.

Frank rode his mare, Tosca, down into México. He crossed the border about fifty miles west of El Paso. He avoided camp fires at night and dust plumes during the day, and, with a fool's luck, managed to pick his way, mostly successfully, between horse thieves from both sides, the Texas rangers who pursued them, Pancho Villa's Dorados, General Pershing's 6,000 gringo troops who were chasing Villa after the raid at Columbus, New Mexico, the Carrancista forces who were maneuvering to block Pershing, weapons smugglers who supplied all sides, common bandits with scars across their eyebrows and twitching hands, private agents

3

who protected the alfalfa and coal supplies, horses, mules, and even locomotives for American and European mining operations and finally the occasional outlaw Apache—banished long since from their tribes for crimes against their own people—who had escaped capture and was now in deep hiding, picking off the odd unwary interloper.

When Frank started out, he had ridden away from armies. He had avoided gullies and canyons where he could be trapped by any of the other groups. He counted on them thinking he was the first scout in a column of mounted soldiers coming along a ridge.

He rode at night so he could see campfires and by day so he could watch for dust plumes and see where he was going. The trouble was, the people he wanted to skirt didn't always make enough dust to give themselves away.

Two weeks into México, he found himself on a ridge looking down on a column of *Carrancistas*—General Carranza's troops.

Two hundred yards away there were a half dozen mounted troopers and three heavy mule-drawn wagons moving across his path from east to west. He backed away, dismounted and tied Tosca to a mesquite bush, then crept forward and dropped onto his stomach. Taking off his hat, he moved rocks into a small pile to support his brass telescope, offsetting the trembling the poisoning caused in his hands. After adjusting the focus he saw a goatherd—a young boy who limped—standing among his goats. Alerted by his dogs, the boy looked right at Frank. Just beyond the boy—over a rise—the mule train bumped along raising dust. He estimated the boy to be about eight years old.

Maybe the dogs barked, maybe a goat bleated. But the officer in charge of the mule train rode toward the boy, who threw stones at the goats to move them toward Frank and away from the wagons, which he could hear but not see. He had chosen Frank as the lesser threat. The officer came over the rise and rode into the herd. He drew his revolver and aimed at a yearling. The boy picked up a rock and threw it at the officer, hitting the man's horse and making it dance. The boy picked up another rock. The dogs barked and snarled and lunged at the horse. The officer raised his revolver. Not at the dogs, but at the boy. Frank put down the telescope, pulled his Winchester up beside him, pushed off the safety, squinted and, without the benefit of magnifying lenses, fired over the long distance.

He had meant it as a warning, but he was not a good shot and with a sinking feeling he realized he might have hit the man. He could not see well enough to be sure. He pressed the telescope to his eye. The officer was halfway out of his saddle, clinging to the horse's mane. He appeared unable to climb back up. He turned the horse in a tight circle, to bring the animal under him. He regained his seat, but he could not sit up straight and slumped over the saddle horn gripping it with both hands, the pistol still in one of them. Then the horse, harassed by the dogs, broke and raced after the mule train.

Frank rose to his knees, upright like a prairie dog. The boy sat on the ground, holding his arm out and with the other hand gripping his armpit, looking up at Frank. The mule train had passed. There was no telling what would happen . . . whether they would stop and ride back or go on.

Frank rode down, dismounted and examined the boy. The officer's bullet had missed his chest, passed through his armpit, and caught the outer edge of the triceps of his right arm, as it left. Frank had not heard the shot. "You should have let him take a goat or two."

"They belong to us," said the boy.

"I'm going to stop the bleeding," said Frank.

He used his bandana as a tourniquet and set the boy in the saddle in front of him. The boy gestured east. The goats flowed in around them. Two dogs led the way, as was their training; two came along behind, holding the herd together. It was the end of the day, and Frank was sure everyone except him knew where he was going.

At the next ridge he stopped and looked back for signs of pursuit. The officer could have fallen from his horse and be bleeding to death, while the wagon column continued west expecting him to catch up. Then again, they must have heard the shots. The wagons were heavy, probably carrying ammunition. Would they dare leave the wagons and come back looking for their officer? For all they knew, the shots had come from Villa's troops or Pershing's gringos or some other group.

Or the officer had made it back but was in too much shock to be coherent about the threat. If he had given some kind of report, how could they be sure it was a lone sniper or even where the shot had come from? His horse had bolted. He hadn't looked back to assess what had happened. There weren't enough of them to guard the mule train and come back looking for him. And so Frank bet they had not followed. On the other hand, the whole Carrancista brigade could be just back over the last ridge.

All of this made Frank's head hurt and his hands tremble. He wished he had not fired at the man. He wished the man had not wanted mutton and then drawn his pistol on a boy who limped. He wished the boy had not thrown stones, or even been there.

He rode higher into the mountains, watching the boy's hand signals. The boy made better path choices for Tosca than the dogs did. They came down through a gap to trees and a village—a few huts made of stone, with crude shingles for roofs—beside a creek. The goats spread out along the banks, nibbling at the green. A young woman with a long black braid appeared in a doorway. She called out to the boy. He gave a weak wave. The woman came faster. Other women came out. They lifted the boy down. Men came and helped Frank down as well, because his shirt was soaked in blood and they thought he was wounded.

The women took Frank and the boy to the creek, carrying the boy and holding Frank on either side. They undressed them—Frank kept his shorts on—and inspected them. They laid hot compresses of aloe vera on the boy's wound. They washed Frank, who sat in the creek letting hands smooth away the blood and look for wounds.

He had not bathed for a long time, and that embarrassed him. He was confused as to who they were, where the men had gone and what had happened to Tosca. But when he turned his head, he saw that she was tied to a pine, eating grass held up to her muzzle by a patient little girl, who was talking to the mare. He was too far away to hear. He wondered in what language she was using: Spanish, one of the Indian languages or both.

The boy's mother came around in front of Frank, standing in the stream. She leaned over and put her palms on his cheeks. At first, Frank flinched. She persisted and gave him a kiss on his forehead. She washed out his shirt and trousers. An older woman, possibly her mother, waded up to him and pointed at his shorts. At first he did not understand. She bent down and tugged at his waist. She rubbed her fists together, to indicate washing. He motioned for her to turn her back. He slipped out of his shorts. Now he sat naked in the stream, even more embarrassed and ill at ease—his modesty protected only by the distortion in water that eddied past him.

The older woman held up his shorts, to show she had made progress. Women on the bank called encouragement. She smiled at him. The smile was warm. *"¡Mejor!"* – "Much better!" she said, and smacked the cloth with her palm.

The boy's mother brought a brown wool blanket and handed it to him. Frank stood up facing the opposite bank and wrapped it around himself. The upside down letters read "U.S. Army 10th Cavalry."

They sat around an outdoor fire and ate bowls of goat meat and tomato soup with pieces of dried *chipotle* floating between islands of fat. That night, they made a straw pallet for Frank in a corner of the stone hut where the boy and his mother lived. The boy, his mother and his grandmother slept on three pallets next to his.

The moon rose and peeked in the door. The temperature dropped. At times, he heard the grandmother cough. Later, out of a dead man's sleep, he opened his eyes. He heard horses, their hooves soft in the dust. He felt a young warm body—the boy's mother—behind him. She laid a hand on his arm and shook him. He stood up naked and hard, picked up the Winchester and walked to the door, slightly hunched—as if that would protect him from danger, from the cold dirt floor, from being naked in front of strangers.

The grandmother, wrapped in a blanket, shuffled over to him. He levered a shell into the chamber. She put a hand on the barrel, lowering it. They were not Carrancistas, she murmured in Spanish. They were not attacking. They were only passing through.

He heard them cross the stream, coming closer. He drew back, away from the door. He counted some thirty horses. The last horse went by. Dust hung in the moonlight. He heard the occasional sound of a rock clicking against another rock, then just the sound of water.

The grandmother went back to her pallet. Frank laid his Winchester beside him and slipped under the U.S. Army blanket. From behind, the mother's warm limbs wrapped around him, then she lay still. Soon he both felt and heard her heavy breathing. Once, as if to orient himself, he reached back. He felt her thick braid and followed it down her bare spine to the round of her buttocks. The grandmother coughed again, farther away. And then he slept.

CHAPTER 2

"Alexander's Ragtime Band"

When his eyes opened he tried to understand where he was. He put his hand out for the Winchester. It was gone. He was alone on the pallet. Two men were talking outside the door. They seemed to be arguing with the grandmother. He heard the word "rifle" and then her saying, "These thing belong to the gringo."

The young woman brought him his clothes. She had been drying them over the fire. They smelled like smoke. He could not read her look. She was taller than her mother, her skin darker, her face broader, with high cheekbones and dark eyebrows. She watched him dress, her glance cast below his waist. He turned his back to her, even though he was pretty sure he had just lain naked against her all night long.

She said the men had come in and taken his rifle. They had found the horse—still saddled—tied to a tree behind the house. They wanted him to follow them. She placed a thick tortilla in his palm, with cold goat meat, sliced avocado and a raw jalapeño.

The men made him walk in front. They marched him around a stone wall, past an old chapel. The side of the chapel was white-washed and had bullet holes in it. That is where they would shoot him, he thought. With his own rifle. The mule kick in the chest. But they went on, in front now, leading Tosca, who turned to look back at him. The two men talked in a mixture of Spanish and something else. It sounded more like conversation than plotting. Frank tossed the taco he'd been carrying away from the path where no one could see it.

They entered a grove of *pirules* where as many as forty horses stood tied up to the trees. There were cooking fires, the sweet smoke of dried *garambullo* cactus they used for fuel. They took him to a medium-sized man, with a mustache and a smirk, who sipped *café de olla* mixed with cinnamon and *piloncillo* from a blue tin cup. In his other hand he held a tortilla with egg and diced prickly pear pads—*nopales*—that were trying to escape from the unfolded end.

"Do you know who I am?" the man asked, leaning against a big rock.

My grandfather Frank did not know.

"I am the *Jefe* of the Division of the North. I just attacked your goddamn Columbus."

"Columbus, Ohio?" Frank asked.

The *Jefe* – Boss – squinted at him, taking in the insolence. Or was it bravery? How could he have guessed mercury poisoning? A frown like a dark moon rose on his forehead.

"No, Columbus, *Nuevo México*, you dumb fucker."

And then, turning to the two men who had brought Frank to the camp, the Jefe said, "Take him to the chapel and shoot him." Then he bit into the open end of the tortilla. "Leave the horse and the rifle and the telescope with me," he added, his mouth full and a piece of nopal stuck on his mustache.

My grandfather said something like the things weren't for sale. That was when the Jefe suspected the young American was stupid, not insolent. For that reason, he was more disposed to listen when the limping boy and the boy's grandmother and mother—the young woman with the long thick braid and the dark eye brows—approached the big rock and told the Jefe that the gringo had shot a Carrancista officer, nearly knocking him off his horse, a Carrancista bastard who was about to shoot the boy, which he did.

The grandmother undid the cloth bandage and revealed the open wound. "Look at this under his arm, not just a nick!" she said. "The gringo fired and saved the boy and brought the boy back to his mother, and he saved the goats, which is probably what you are eating right now, since your men took two of them during the night."

The Jefe held up his hand and said, "All right, all right, sit down." He gestured to Frank as well. "And have something to eat." Then he turned his eyes on the boy's mother, and his eyes got glassy and interested.

The grandmother thanked the Jefe for the invitation, wished him *buen provecho,* and said they were sure his men would not take more goats from poor people who needed all of them up to and including their ears just to survive. Then they took the gringo's mare, the Winchester and the spyglass, plus the gringo—who they said was a guest of the people of the mountains—and the boy back to their hut.

The boy's mother, this time with the boy as well, got back under the U.S. Army blanket with Frank. Tosca, now inside as well—tied to the two finger holes in the door—occasionally thumped her hooves on the dirt floor.

Everyone slept till the sun was high and the chickens had laid enough for another meal. Something other than goat meat.

After splashing water on their faces, they sat in the shade of a pine next to the stream on three-legged stools made of mesquite, and ate *huevos revueltos* from dented plates while listening to the water whisper in the stream.

Frank looked up. The same two men, now mounted, appeared at the top of the trail in a cloud of dust and flies. They were trying to decide something. Perhaps another raid on the horse, rifle and telescope. They rode down toward them. No one got up. Frank, they said, was to go with them again. There was nothing to worry about. Their eyes said they believed what they were saying. Maybe not completely, but close to it. And then they waited.

Frank slipped on his boots, set his old canvas hat on his head and brought Tosca out of the hut. The saddle creaked when he swung his leg over and settled. He turned and looked at his hosts.

"We're coming right behind you," said the grandmother.

The horses stumbled up the trail, past the whitewashed wall of the chapel . . . and the bullet holes. They came into the *pirul* grove. Six men were entering from the other side. Slung by ropes between them was an upright piano, approaching like a small elephant. They set it down. They ran empty grain sacks over the chipped varnish to clear away the dust. The Jefe took a position beside the piano, his arms at his side—a schoolboy standing at attention. A German photographer—so they said—dressed in dirty white linen but mostly hidden under a black cloak, held a narrow pan above his head. There was a flash and a lot of white smoke. Two soldiers led the German to his mule. They helped him pack his gear and mount and led him away. He was not to photograph anything else. A frown formed on the Jefe's brow. One of the escorts tapped Frank on the shoulder.

"He wants you to play. We found your music."

When Frank had ridden from Mogollón to Silver City to file mining claims for his father, Edwin, he often sang arias. He was an enthusiastic tenor with a limited range. Tosca had often heard him belt out arias from *La Traviata* and *La Bohème*—Puccini's "Che gelida manina" from *La Bohème,* his favorite. He had left the music in his saddlebags.

The escorts pushed him forward, holding Tosca for him. The boy, his mother and his grandmother arrived. The mother took Tosca's reins. She nodded at Frank. She would watch over his telescope and rifle. His escort pushed him again. The Jefe pointed at the piano. "Play it."

Frank saw no stool. He made a squatting motion with his body. Everyone laughed, including the boy and his mother, because it resembled something else. The Jefe grabbed one of the escorts by the neck and forced him down onto his hands and knees. Frank sat on him. He sat where the spine and the pelvis joined, where he estimated the chair was the strongest. He hadn't tried to play the piano in a year or two. The distance between the dusty keys and *La Bohème* seemed equal to the distance he had traveled. He plunked out a few notes. Maybe the mercury protected him from the fear he should have felt. He tried to remember "Drink to Me Only with Thine Eyes". Everyone stared at him, some with their mouths open, yearning for something they couldn't quite remember, but that would come out of the piano.

Perhaps inspired by the earlier reprieve or perhaps by the long raven-black braid of the young mother who held Tosca, Frank finally began to play, stumbling at first, working around the sticking keys, until the strains, unrecognizable at first, then clearer and clearer, of "Alexander's Ragtime Band"—music both sweet and universal—came out of the piano. The song had become popular in 1911, and everyone present could imagine himself dancing under Japanese or Porfirian lanterns, with women in long white dresses, or with men in *charro* suits and sombreros and handsome mustaches who never hit women and had warm adoring eyes—everyone full of hope and longing. The women who cooked and tended the Jefe's men, who smelled of pepper from the grove, glided forward from the trees to listen.

Frank played it through once. He looked up. The General— that's what his men called the Jefe—wagged his finger at him metronome-style. I am warning you, said his eyes, just this side of dangerous. Don't make us feel that way. Make us feel that way again, and I'll hang you from the closest *pirul*. Then he made a circular motion with his forefinger.

"*La misma.*" – Play it again, not a different one. Play it again.

Frank played. Each time, the General made the sign with his forefinger. Each time, Frank played it again. Maybe eight times before riders broke into the clearing, filling the concert hall with dust and shouting. Everyone mounted. The General barked orders. Then the riders struck off down the path. Men without horses ran behind them with their rifles, weighed down by bandoliers of ammunition, and disappeared behind a wall of dust.

Frank stood at the piano. The boy and his mother led Tosca to him. She handed him the reins, then turned and led the boy away. When Frank tried to follow, she picked up a stone and threw it at him. It missed. Tosca balked. When he followed again, she threw another stone, harder this time, with tears in her eyes. Neither the boy nor Frank understood.

He followed them to the hut, coming along behind, out of range. She shut the door behind her. He sat by the stream and let Tosca eat the green grass at the edge of the bank. When he went up to the hut, he found tortillas and goat meat wrapped in a cloth, sitting on the rock step. When he knocked, she did not open. Maybe it had something to do with the music. He did not even know her name. He saw the boy looking at him through a finger hole.

At dusk, he tightened Tosca's cinch and rode south along the stream until the trail climbed and crossed an open ridge. The moon came up and put their shadows ahead of them, leading them south. He did not ride far. He camped in a grove of *pirules,* on a soft floor of old dry manure from animals that had taken shade there. He kept Tosca saddled, in case he needed to leave quickly. He wrapped himself in his wool blanket, with his Winchester in his arms.

The air smelled like pepper. He missed the young mother's warm body against his back. In the morning, on a flat rock, he found, wrapped in cloth, two tortillas filled with avocado, chiles and hard boiled egg—and two stones, throwing size. *Maybe these are for you if you come back. Maybe these are for you if you don't come back.*

CHAPTER 3

Mr. Leibniz and the Avocado

Frank rode east through the Los Arados mountains and fell in with a well-bred, older señora, who was polite but formal and standoffish. She was traveling with three of her ranch hands, who were well-armed and watchful. She had been visiting her brother in Progreso—a remote village in the middle of nowhere in the state of Chihuahua. Now, together with Frank, they rode down the long slopes toward the Chihuahua-El Paso rail line at El Sueco.

Frank used his telescope to survey the sleepy train station. Heat waves distorted the images he was looking at. They passed the glass back and forth, discussing the safety of approaching. There was no sign of troops. Corpses hung from the telegraph poles a quarter mile in either direction. They waited under a mesquite tree closer in. The horses swished away flies and thumped the dust. The black hands on Frank's silver watch crept past the hour twice. Then they saw smoke on the northern horizon. The train pulled in and began taking on coal and water.

They hired a girl selling candied sweet potatoes—*camotes*—to walk the length of the train and report back to them. There were no soldiers, she reported. No army horses. Just cattle, in three cars, twenty or so passengers in another car up ahead so they wouldn't smell the cattle and the three unsaddled horses in the last car.

The girl then came up to Frank. She asked him if he'd like to hear them whistle.

"Who?" said Frank.

"Them," she said, and pointed up the line to the hanging corpses. "You tap them on their feet and it makes them whistle."

Frank stared at her.

"Out of their mouths," she said.

A bent man with a limp threw down a ramp from the last car. The señora's cowboys — *vaqueros* — ran their five horses up into the car and tied them to a gnawed rail.

The ranch hands stayed with the horses. Frank and the señora found a place on a wooden seat in the passenger car. The young man across from them had fine features, thoughtful eyes and a full black mustache. A boy of about three was stretched on his lap asleep. The boy's drool made a dark spot on the man's trousers.

The train jerked forward. The cracked window let in the warm afternoon air. The señora's head nodded forward and after a while she slept.

Frank and the young man across from him fell into conversation . . . in English. Juan Carlos was from Morelia. He had studied medicine in London for four years and had planned to be a doctor, but now he was not so sure. He asked Frank if he was familiar with the concept of parallelism. Frank shook his head.

"The German philosopher Leibniz says that a decision and the act that follows are two parallel events that God causes, and that there is no causal interaction between the decision and the act."

Frank nodded, but did not understand.

"But that leaves the question of responsibility," Juan Carlos said. "Are we responsible for our acts?"

Frank nodded again.

"I will give you an example. I caught this train in El Paso. The train is slow. Two days ago it came to a halt for a long time.

Near dawn in the middle of this high desert, a hundred and forty kilometers north of here, in El Lucero. I was about to get down onto the tracks when the train slowly began to jolt forward. Then it paused again. This happened repeatedly. Finally, I climbed down onto the rail bed, stretched, and looked around.

"The eastern light threw a soft pink mist over the entire landscape. Except for the occasional hiss of the steam escaping from the engine, everything was quiet. The desert gave off that wonderful smell of greasewood, and I felt a sudden joy to be back in México. I could smell wood smoke. I assumed it was from the modest shelters along the rail line. I walked forward, easily keeping pace with the train, until it stopped completely. I heard horses and saw cooking fires, then a sea of men, some lying down and some standing.

"I squatted and looked under the train. There were men and horses on the other side of the train as well. They were soldiers. They stared at the train, but seemed uninterested in approaching it. No one seemed to move. No one walked anywhere. The horses were hobbled, and they were trying to graze on the desert floor. I realized that many of the men lying on the ground had had their shoes removed and were dead or dying. Horses lay in pools of dark blood. Once in a while they tried to raise their heads. No one was bothering to put them down. Perhaps because there was no ammunition left.

"There was a musky smell, different from other dead things. I knew it from working with cadavers in my medical studies. It was mixed with the smell of human shit, but also that of beans and coffee.

"There was a sound like a wind in the telegraph lines, but there was no wind. Plus a lower register of rocks clicking together, which I realized were dry throats trying to call out, summoning a doctor, the saints or a mother.

"In a half an hour, we had passed most of the soldiers, both dead and alive. They were my countrymen—Carrancistas, Villistas, counter-revolutionary Huertistas or Orozcistas. I had no idea which. I was about to board the train when I saw a woman. She was dressed like a man in an army blouse and trousers. But I could tell by the hips. I angled off toward her.

"She was some sort of angel of mercy. I was curious to know how she was helping the wounded. I began to realize my own obligation to help. I could see she was really quite lovely. I was about to greet her when I saw the quick motion she made while bending over a wounded soldier. He raised his hand in gratitude, and then the knife moved, and she cut him from ear to ear and spoke to him with what appeared to be words of comfort.

"She walked from man to man. She worked quickly. She seemed to be choosing the young men.

"I began to run. She had reached her third or so when I got to her. I called out. She did not seem to hear me. She cut the boy right in front of me. I thought of taking the knife from her, but I knew she would just pick up one of the bayonets lying all around us. I got in front of her. I asked her what she was doing. She stopped. She was lovely. A rare beauty. She looked educated and spoke that way. She said war was evil and that she would put an end to it. I told her the young soldiers were swept up in something they did not understand and were innocent. She said I was handsome and when she was through we would make love under a mesquite tree that was thirty or so meters away. As she talked, spittle collected in one corner of her mouth. She pushed by me.

"I picked up the rifle that was lying next to the boy she had just murdered. We had reached the edge of the battlefield, and the locomotive engineer had decided it was safe to accelerate. I did not know what to do. There was the whole other side of the tracks, another whole field of wounded. An officer might come along and stop her, but how many would she slaughter before that? I hit her between the shoulder blades with the butt of the rifle. She fell forward, then snarled like a dog, rolled around and slashed back and forth at my legs with the knife while getting to her feet. She lunged at me. I hit her in the forehead with the steel-capped butt of the rifle. I was bathed in sweat. The smell of some kind of cologne, like rosewater, hung in the air. She spun away from me and fell face down. As if in a dream, and as if I had been highly trained, I reversed the rifle and drove its bayonet through her back just below the left scapula all the way into the ground, so it stood there when I took my hands away.

"In the meantime, the train had accelerated. I ran toward it and barely reached it. The last thing I did was pick up this boy who knelt clinging to a dead soldier. He fought me and screeched that I was taking him from his father. I shouted back at him, did he have any family? He shook his head, and so I took him . . . and here we are," Juan Carlos said, glancing down at the child on his lap and then up at Frank, as if waiting for judgment.

"So, tell me. Who was responsible in this case, me or God?"

Frank had no answer. He thought of the hanging corpses that would whistle when you tapped their feet. That seemed more like God's work.

The señora stirred and brought her head up. She glanced at the two young men and saw the sunken, pained eyes of the one and the puzzlement on the forehead of the other.

"Is everything alright?" she asked. "Would you like me to take the child for a while?" She did not wait for an answer. She got up and sat down beside Juan Carlos and carefully pulled the boy over onto her own lap. Then she took out a soft cotton handkerchief and dabbed at his sweaty forehead.

"We were discussing whether we are responsible for our actions," said Juan Carlos.

"We most assuredly are," she said, looking up from the child. "I'm afraid I was half listening. You will make a fine doctor and that's the end of it."

She looked at Frank. "There are three avocados in my satchel if you don't mind rummaging. And a spoon. We'll save one for the boy. Mr. Leibniz is not here, so he will not need one. In my half-sleep I have determined that I do not wish to have either of you swinging from telegraph poles or standing in front of some firing squad made up of mescal-muddled soldiers who are so hungry they can hardly stand. In Chihuahua you will both come to my house. With the boy. And we will see what needs to be done from there."

CHAPTER 4

The Boy, the Fly, and the Avocado

Juan Carlos took a silver flask out of his satchel, filled its cap and offered it to the señora, who smiled and shook her head. She gestured toward Frank, who drank the whiskey and handed the cap back. Juan Carlos drank a capful and returned the flask to his satchel. The whiskey had its effect, and Frank and Juan Carlos took their turns at drowsing, their heads bowing forward, their shoulders touching.

When Frank raised his head, he saw the boy on the señora's lap, and the señora looking across at him nodding that he should keep on sleeping. He felt a rare sense of safety and peace with her and the child in front of him and Juan Carlos at his side asleep, leaning slightly against him. He thought about duality—a term he had once heard—about separateness and togetherness and about the rare moments of trust between men—almost an animal trust—when strangers give each other comfort. He thought of his father and saw his face . . . with one cheek shot off by a Confederate musket ball. He remembered him saying once that you could lie next to your wife for twenty years and not really know her completely. Yet, that lying against each other night after night was a complete closeness and the basis of real friendship between a man and a woman. Knowing her was not always possible and not even necessary, if there was friendship and respect.

Frank thought he understood that for the first time, and it might be true between men as well. That friendship might be possible by the mere touching of shoulders between complete strangers on a train, in the late afternoon, on the hard wooden seats, with the smell of coal smoke from the engine ahead, the swaying car, the rhythm of the wheels over the rail joints, the pulse of the pistons and the forward movement.

He was with an older woman he did not know, who was holding a child she did not know and he did not know. They were together, some touching, others not, shifting on their seats, exchanging nods and smiles, and looks, all gentle . . . except when his Winchester fell over and startled them. Then they talked a little about the boy who had been rescued—or abducted—from a battlefield. They did not know which.

The sun moved lower in the western sky, casting shadows. The passing countryside grew golden. The boy, still on the señora's lap, woke up, opened his eyes but did not move. His shirt and trousers had been mended and patched many times. His arms and legs were thin. Frank followed his gaze and saw he was watching a fly on the window. The fly walked up. Then down. Then sideways. Then up again. Then he saw the boy was looking at him.

The señora realized the boy was awake and gathered him in a little closer. She offered him water from her canteen. He pressed his lips together and would not drink. With her permission, Frank took the third avocado from the señora's satchel. He worked the yellow-handled penknife his grandfather had given him out of his pocket, opened it and cut the avocado in half. He pressed the sharp edge of the blade against the pit, cutting into it until he could lift it out. He worked the knife blade away from the pit. He held up the pit so the boy could see it. Then, he slipped the pit through the opening in the window and let it drop.

"I just planted a tree," he said. The señora smiled. The boy's eyes widened.

He showed the boy his empty hand. He held up his penknife and he folded it closed. The boy watched everything. Juan Carlos was awake . . . watching the magic show, which consisted of nothing more than Frank opening and closing his jackknife.

Frank handed Juan Carlos the spoon and half of the avocado. Juan Carlos scooped out a little on the tip of the spoon and touched the boy's lips with it. The boy kept his lips together. Juan Carlos handed the avocado and the spoon to the señora. She touched the boy's lips with the spoon, and he slowly opened his mouth and took the food.

The boy chewed for a while, then swallowed. Then he watched the fly for a while. The señora held the water where he could see it. He turned his head toward the canteen. The señora handed the spoon and avocado to Frank. She pulled out the canteen's cork stopper, sat the boy upright with his back to her, and he drank, clutching the canteen with his small dusty hands. While he drank, he looked at the fly. Then he looked at Frank, who sat across from him.

Frank carved out another spoonful of avocado and held it a few inches in front of the boy's lips. The boy watched Frank but did not lean forward. Frank gave the spoon to the señora. She held it to the boy's lips.

As if it were routine, he opened his mouth and ate, then indicated he wanted more water, then watched the fly for a while, then looked over to see what was left of the avocado in Frank's hand.

The señora reached out and gave the spoon back to Frank. He loaded it and held it out again. This time, the boy leaned forward and took the food. As he chewed, he and Frank watched the fly. The boy turned his head and looked at Juan Carlos, who by now was dozing again with his head sunk forward. The boy pointed at Juan Carlos. Frank smiled and nodded. Yes, Juan Carlos was sleeping while the rest of them were awake.

The señora splashed a little water on her handkerchief and washed the boy's hands. The child leaned back against her breast. His lids grew heavy. She laid him across her lap and, in time, his drooling began again, making a widening dark spot on the outline of her thigh.

When night fell, men took turns, two at a time, riding on the cow-catcher at the front of the locomotive, holding lanterns close to the rails, looking for wires, explosives and other signs of sabotage. The conductor, a thin man with a hawk nose, hung a red lantern on the last car so they would not be rammed from the rear by a fast moving military train. Another lantern, with clear glass and a yellow flame, hung from the ceiling in the middle of the passenger car. It was cold outside, so they kept the windows shut. The air reeked of kerosene fumes. They slept as best they could, lying down where there was space on the hard seats, slumped in the corners, or just nodding forward.

CHAPTER 5

The Wounded Man

The boy slept through the night. Eventually the stars faded, and the sky dawned gray. The train slowed to a stop where food sellers stood beside the tracks. The engineer and his fireman each unhooked a blue cup, climbed down from the engine and approached a woman who stood behind a pot of *atole.* The trainmen fished coins out of their pockets and held out their cups for the hot *atole.*

There were various kinds of grasses for horses and cattle. The vaqueros walked past and waved. The cattle agent got down and began bargaining with the women for the hay.

Frank opened the window so they could hear. The engineer was asking questions. What did they know about the line ahead? Who were they likely to run into? Had people blown up the tracks? When did the last train come through? Were they likely to meet a train coming toward them—military or otherwise? Did they know the positions of the various armies and their suppliers?

The answers were confusing and contradictory. Was there information by telegraph?

"No, as you can see," said the woman selling *atole,* "the lines were cut everywhere."

Were the sidings ahead of them occupied, torn up, or otherwise inaccessible? Was there water for the engine, as well as for the horses and cattle? Was there coal? Was there wood, in case there wasn't coal? What about bandits?

There were bandits, the women reported, if that meant groups of foraging ex-soldiers—bands of Villistas who had gone home but found no jobs—who were now using their guns to provide for their families.

At the next stop, the señora walked with the boy to the back of the train to visit the horses and check on her three escorts. They had come forward at intervals during the night to check on her. Now they slept on their backs on the hay except for Samuel, the head man, who watched them with one eye, then closed it again . . . satisfied that everything was fine.

The boy held her hand tightly and did not speak. As they walked, she pointed out various types of cactus growing near the tracks. He pointed at a lavender-colored flower—with lacy leaves—growing out of the rail bed gravel.

"Cosmos," said the señora.

"*Flor muerte*," said the boy. Then he had to pee and turned away. At first she did not help him, but in the end, squatted behind him, reached between his legs and held his trousers back out of the way so he didn't wet them.

They returned to the passenger car. The boy had some *atole* and then fell asleep. The engine pulled forward. Two men sat forward just above the cow-catcher so they could see the tracks better. At eight or so in the morning, they entered a green area, with ash and oak trees and pasture. A group of armed horsemen stood on one side of the tracks, far up the line. The train slowed to a crawl, then stopped, still several hundred yards away.

The engineer was debating what to do. The line was perfectly straight. By leaning out the window a little, Frank could see the horsemen. He saw peaked military hats. But that could mean anything. They might or might not be part of a standing army.

Military clothing was plentiful and could have been stripped from corpses. But, these men were dressed to a man like the officer Frank had shot.

Besides his own, Frank had seen a few other rifles in the car. The señora's men each had one. That was four. When he looked around, he saw two passengers standing in the corridor. Each of them held a rifle. "I count six," said Juan Carlos.

"Six, at least," said Frank.

They might be able to defend against twenty experienced riders. But it was not clear whether the two other passengers knew how to use their rifles. Frank wasn't even sure about himself.

They walked forward along the train on the side away from the riders. Frank looked back once and saw the señora's men coming along behind them carrying their rifles.

The engineer stood back as Frank and Juan Carlos climbed the steel ladder to the cab. He greeted them, but with a frown. They asked him what he thought of the situation. His young fireman stood to one side. He held his right wrist in the air in front of him. The hand was bent downward. His left foot was turned inward. His face lit up when they greeted them, but then he turned away, as if the difference in his limbs denied him the right to an opinion.

"We have six rifles," said Juan Carlos.

The engineer shook his head. Frank didn't know what that meant. Not enough rifles or the situation was hopeless. Or, maybe he didn't fight armies.

"We could reverse," said Juan Carlos. The driver looked at him without reacting.

Samuel, the señora's head man, climbed up. "Do we have enough coal and water to run right through them?"

The driver said they didn't. This was where they had to stop. This was where the water was . . . and maybe coal.

Standing back from the engineer's window on the left side, Frank studied the riders with the telescope. "They're dressed cleanly," he said.

"Carrancistas," said the engineer.

Holding the boy's hand, the señora had come up along the hidden side of the train. Samuel looked down at her. "I'm thinking, we put armed men on top of the cars," he called down. "Three over the passenger car and three over the last car . . . they will think better of attacking us if we approach slowly and show we are suspicious but not aggressive. That's my recommendation."

"I agree," said the señora. The driver nodded his head. The señora and the boy walked back to their car.

It turned out, there were nine, not six, rifles. Four other passengers agreed to climb on top of the passenger car. The señora's men got up on the last car, above the horses. One more passenger joined them. Frank and Juan Carlos stayed in the locomotive. Frank had his Winchester in his hand and a box of shells in his over-the-shoulder canvas satchel.

"Stay completely out of sight," said Juan Carlos. "There is no way to explain who you are. Gun smuggler, U.S. agent, mercenary or even a gringo Villista."

The train pulled forward, hissing from its pistons in slow intervals, as if it were thinking. The mounted soldiers had drawn out their rifles. They held them vertically, with the butts on their thighs. The posture was cautionary, not necessarily aggressive. The train came to a stop in front of the water tower and the coaling platform.

No one spoke. The stationmaster's helper, a man with a notch cut out of one ear, swung the canvas water hose over the tender. While the water fell, he shoveled coal into the locomotive's coal bin, an area in front of the locomotive's water tank. Frank drew back into a nook between the water compartment and the landing shovelfuls of coal. With each thump, black dust rose, darkening his face and hands. Drops of water from the water hose above him gave him white moles. All of this to the amusement of the stoker with the crooked limbs, who smiled with perfect white teeth at Frank's transformation.

None of the horsemen had dismounted. No one was trying to board the train. An officer rode up to the cab and called to the engineer. Frank watched him through an opening no bigger than a man's eye. The officer was light-skinned, mustached and aristocratic. Through another opening, Frank saw people unloading a stretcher from what looked like a military wagon. A man in uniform lay on the stretcher. His face was ashen. A grey blanket covered his body. Blood from what appeared to be a thigh wound seeped up through the cover, making a dark stain. The two bearers placed the stretcher on the ground. The mounted officer gestured toward the south. He had to raise his voice to be heard over the falling coal and the hiss of steam. "Can you take him to Chihuahua?"

"Can I get through?" the engineer shouted back.

"We control the line," said the officer.

"And who are you?" the engineer asked.

"The Constitutionalist Army of President Carranza. And you? Who are your passengers?"

"Civilian travelers," Juan Carlos prompted, to the back of the engineer's head.

"Civilian travelers," said the engineer.

"How many?"

"About thirty," the engineer lied.

"Who are the men on the top of the cars?"

"We weren't sure who you were."

"We are the Constitutionalist Federal Army," said the officer, and he spurred his horse forward a bit, to size up Juan Carlos who was still standing behind the engineer.

"Who is that?" he asked.

Juan Carlos stepped forward. "Juan Carlos Soros Adame, at your service. I am a medical student returning to Morelia. I've been studying in England."

"Why are you in the cab?" the officer asked, as if he had not heard the first part.

"I like locomotives. All the levers and valves. To see how it all works."

The officer thought about that. Juan Carlos watched his face, to see whether the brow wrinkled or the mouth hardened. He saw both skepticism and credulity, alternating, like the sun disappearing behind a cloud and then coming out again.

"We need to put him up in the passenger car, except his leg smells bad," said the officer, pointing at the man on the stretcher.

"Put him in the last car," said Juan Carlos, assuming the role of doctor. "There's hay. The car is more open. He'll be more comfortable."

"Can you look after him?" the officer asked.

Juan Carlos nodded his head. "I will do my best."

With his coal-dust-covered right hand, Frank slowly released the hammer of his Winchester so that it rested safely on the firing pin. He checked the opposite side of the train. The Carrancista horsemen, who at one point had ridden around to that side, had now returned to the station side. He crossed the engine floor and stood so that he would be hidden behind Juan Carlos. The officer and the stretcher bearers had moved down the train to the last car. They were loading the wounded man. Apparently, they were sending him on alone, with nothing more than a canteen of water and his grey, blood-soaked blanket. Then the cavalry squad rode around the back of the train. Frank and Juan Carlos crossed the steel floor of the cab, so they could watch. They saw the horsemen heading off west at a slow canter. Frank counted them. Twenty men. They had all left, taking the wagon team with them.

CHAPTER 6

Aloe Vera, Green String

The coaling and watering took another half hour. A woman with a face crumpled from leprosy walked alongside the train selling tamales. She used leather-hinged wooden tongs to hand up four husk-wrapped tamales, one at a time, to the señora, who tied them up in her bandana.

Juan Carlos walked to the horse car to check on the wounded man. He passed male passengers, who stood around smoking. Woman chatted with one another. Frank washed coal dust from his hands and face, using water from the overflow tub under the watering hose. He removed his canvas hat and smoothed water over the top of his head. The conductor signed the invoice. The locomotive driver gave a short blast on the whistle. Everyone returned to their seats, Juan Carlos coming last. He reported that the wounded man was an officer, he was not doing well, and there wasn't much he, Juan Carlos, could do for him other than clean his bullet wound and make sure he got enough water.

AS THE TRAIN PULLED WAY, they passed a young priest hanging from a telegraph pole. The lines had been cut and one of them used to hang him. His face was black from trauma and long exposure to the sun. Frank wondered why the people at the coaling station had not cut him down, and he held his breath until he was sure they had left the smell behind.

He sat in his place beside the window, facing toward the back of the train. He stood his rifle in a corner near the window. The señora watched him. "I don't even know your name," he said. "My name is Frank Holloway."

"My name is Mariana. I will not trouble you with the rest of my names. I gather Americans don't understand long names, or which one is which. You can call me Doña Mariana. That will be the easiest thing."

Then everyone looked at the boy, who sat next to the window, across from Frank. The boy did not look at them. "What about you, little one?" Doña Mariana asked. The boy continued looking out the window.

"I'm hungry," he said, in a low, soft voice.

"I have tamales," said Doña Mariana. "First tell me your name, then we will eat."

"My father called me Lito," he said, nearly inaudibly.

"Manuelito?"

The boy nodded.

"Well, that's what I will call you, too. I have two kinds of tamales, Manuelito. One with meat, she explained, and one with cheese and strips of pickled *jalapeño* chile – *rajas.*

"Which would you like?"

"My father liked cheese," said Manuelito, in a small voice.

"Then why don't you have cheese," said Doña Mariana.

Toward noon, they stopped where a siding branched off. A man with a red flag motioned the train into the siding, where they waited for nearly an hour. People got off to stretch their legs. Juan Carlos visited the patient. Finally, the man with the red flag played several wavering blasts on an old bugle and told everyone to get back on board. A military train was approaching, and citizens were not allowed to stand near the tracks.

Juan Carlos sat down and suggested that Frank exchange seats with him, so he would be sitting farther away from the window and be less visible. The car grew quiet as they listened for the approaching train. The open window began to vibrate, then rattle in its grooves. The Winchester's steel barrel, still propped against the windowsill after Frank switched seats, began to dance sideways. Juan Carlos rescued it and handed it to Frank, who laid it below the wooden bench he was sitting on. The whole car began to vibrate, making the Winchester slither along the floor. Frank put his foot on it and pinned it down until the military train had passed.

Troops rode on the top of the passing train. He saw flatcars carrying field cannons, and he counted six as they flew past. He held his old canvas hat so that it partly covered his face. He was still thinking about cannons when he realized it was quiet again.

"I wonder where they're going," Juan Carlos asked.

"Where we just came from," said Doña Mariana. "That is the shortest way to go west toward Patton and Villa." She unwrapped a cold *tamal con queso* and broke off a third for the boy.

"Who is Patton?" Frank asked.

Juan Carlos and the señora gaped at him, as if he had asked what north was.

Manuelito took a bite of the *tamal.* "He's a pilot," he said.

"What's a pilot," Juan Carlos asked.

"Airplanes," said the boy.

"Is that what your father said?" Juan Carlos asked.

Manuelito nodded and continued eating. He plucked out a piece of chile, examined it, then slid it between his lips and started chewing.

In the afternoon the train stopped at a village—some ten houses built along a creek that had no water. The locomotive driver walked toward one of the houses. A woman sold him a cup of something strong enough to make him cock his head sideways like a chicken.

Juan Carlos said he should see to the wounded man again. Frank walked to the last car with him, carrying his Winchester. Doña Mariana's vaqueros were standing on the tracks. They were smoking and talking. Once in a while, they scuffed the gravel rail bed with their boots. They held their rifles in the crooks of their arms and scanned the landscape, seldom looking at one another.

Frank and Juan Carlos climbed up into the boxcar. Frank checked on Tosca. There was clean water in a bucket hooked over a peg near her head, and the vaqueros had tied a bunch of alfalfa so she could pull at it, showing her the same care they gave their own horses.

The wounded man lay on his back in a corner away from the horses. He held his blanket bunched up against his jaw. He was unshaven, his face gray, his eyes weak. The blood that had soaked into his blanket was old and black. A canteen lay within reach. Juan Carlos helped him drink, took his pulse, felt his forehead and passed his hands back and forth across his eyes . . . to check the pupils' dilation, he said. He pulled away the blanket . . . slowly. Someone had cut open the man's trousers and underwear to get at the wound, so he was able to untie the bandage wrapped around the man's upper thigh. The bandage was soaked through, yellow where it had lain against the wound. Both the officer's legs trembled.

"I'm cold," he said.

"You have a fever," said Juan Carlos. "You need to drink. Your pulse is still good. I will find something to change your bandage with."

Frank stayed with the patient and covered him with the blanket again to keep him warm. He held the canteen of water up to the man's lips. The man drank a little. His lips were dry like leather and couldn't form around the edge of the opening. The water ran over his chin and darkened the front of his military blouse.

"You are an American?" he rasped, in English.

"Yes," said Frank.

"I thought so," he said. "You with Pershing?"

"No," said Frank.

"Villa?"

Frank shook his head.

"Then why are you here?" the man asked.

Frank didn't really have an answer.

The man's eyes closed, as if the few words had exhausted him. "Did the bullet go all the way through?"

Frank didn't know, so he didn't answer. Frank estimated that the man was a little older than him. The round collar of his uniform was unbuttoned. It was made of linen—material finer than what the average soldier wore. "You are an officer?" Frank asked.

"Yes."

"A Carrancista?"

The man opened his eyes, as if to see what significance this information might have for Frank. Frank didn't really know what a Carrancista was. "You were in a battle?" Frank asked.

"No," said the officer. "In the middle of nowhere."

"An accident?" Frank asked.

"*Emboscada*" – "An ambush."

He was square-jawed, with very short hair, dark eyebrows, light-skinned and a plunging Roman nose. *A handsome man,* Frank thought.

In a short while, Juan Carlos returned to the boxcar with a fresh leaf of aloe vera and a length of cloth torn from a bedsheet. With his knife, he cut lengthwise down the center of the aloe vera leaf; then turning each section on edge, cut vertically along each fleshy, wet edge, opening each piece into a flat piece that was wet on one side and dry on the other.

He drew away the blanket again and gently cleaned the wound with one of the flat pieces of the aloe vera. Then he turned the man over and used the other piece to clean where the bullet had exited. Then he made a new bandage with the cloth.

Frank helped by moving the patient this way and that as Juan Carlos wrapped the bandage. They made a pillow out of hay and the remaining section of the sheet to make the patient comfortable.

Frank climbed down from the boxcar. Doña Mariana and Manuelito were coming back from their walk along the *arroyo*. The boy spoke to her in short bursts and kept watching her, as if expecting a response. Doña Mariana answered him, but did not look at him. She saw Frank, but gave no greeting. Frank descended the slope and helped her up to the tracks.

"We saw a dog," said Manuelito. "It smelled." They walked toward the passenger car. "It had a green string around its neck," he said.

Doña Mariana gave Frank a look. They climbed the iron steps at the front end of the car. She made a pillow out of her canvas riding hat and had the boy lie down on it. She and Frank chatted a bit about the village, its poverty, the dusty paths and the possible reasons for the train's stopping. The boy's lids grew heavy and soon his mouth relaxed, and he was asleep.

The señora's eyes rested on Frank. "How is the wounded man?" she asked.

"He needs a doctor."

"I think he has one," she said.

"He needs a hospital." Then, after a pause, "You walked up the *arroyo*?"

She said, "Yes," then looked out the window and said nothing else.

"And the green string?" Frank asked. Then he looked out the window toward the *arroyo,* as if he might see the dog.

"Farther back, at the base of an old wall, there are trees and shade and pools of clear standing water. I listened for the train whistle. We didn't want to get left behind. The place reminded me of *arroyos* when I was a child. Peaceful, enchanted places, out of the hot sun, with just the barest sound of water. We always looked for pools to swim in. The perfect pool, in a spot of sun to warm us when we got out.

"When we started back toward the train, we saw the dog. A large dog. And probably friendly, because someone had been able to lift it up and hold it while someone else tied the rope, string really, to the tree. It took two people to do it, at least one of them strong. Its rear feet were able to touch the ground. The green string tightened. The creature struggled to hold itself up, but left alone, eventually slowly choked to death from its own weight."

Frank looked at her.

"There were two men watching us from up above, where the houses are. As if they were waiting for our reaction. I looked back at them longer than I would have ever done with strangers, let alone men. I wanted to see if they were the killers."

She paused again.

"I could not tell. There was nothing in their eyes to indicate whether they had done it." She stopped again, as if considering.

"That is what troubled me. That you couldn't tell one way or the other. All you could see was indifference. I called up to them and said there was a hanged dog and that they should bury it before it brought disease to the village. There was no reaction at all, as if that didn't matter. At that point, I did not want to be there any longer, so we left quickly."

Frank didn't know what to say. Instead, he took his Winchester from the corner by the window and laid it across his lap. He formed his right hand around the stock. His trigger finger lay across the trigger guard and twitched like a wasp. The gun felt solid in his hands. The gun metal of the barrel had dulled. He wondered where he would be able to buy oil and a cloth so he could treat the gun the way it needed to be treated. He worked the lever, just enough to see the brass ring of the chambered round, but only enough so it didn't eject and the next round move into place.

CHAPTER 7

The Icehouse

Later, as they waited, a heavy two-mule wagon creaked up to the locomotive with a load of mesquite wood and dried—still very prickly—*garambullo* cactus.

The train set off again and ran through the night. The conductor came forward carrying a worn long-barreled pistol in his hand. He went and sat below the headlight at the front of the engine, just behind the cow-catcher. The trick was to fire the pistol as a warning, if he saw torn up tracks and the train had to stop. When he was exhausted, other men, including Frank and Juan Carlos, took turns.

A good hour before dawn, the engine ran out of water and stopped a mile outside of Chihuahua.

The engineer and his young fireman set off to look for water, the first with long smooth strides, the second—because of his inward-turned foot—like a small boat bucking a turbulent sea. The conductor poured more kerosene in the red lantern and hung it again on the back of the last car. He placed a second red lantern ahead of the engine, down the line toward Chihuahua, to give a northbound train more warning.

The other passengers waited for the engineer and the fireman to return from their search for water to take them all the way to the city. The señora's head vaquero came forward and said finding water could take a very long time, getting it out of a stream and into a tank, then hauling it by team to the train.

Doña Mariana walked the boy back to the last car and watched as her men unloaded the five horses.

She mounted, and one of her vaqueros handed up Manuelito, whom she settled in front of her. After some discussion, they decided to mount the wounded officer in front of Ricardo, the vaquero with the strongest horse. Juan Carlos rode on Tosca behind Frank. To make more room, Frank unstrapped the Winchester scabbard and held it across his lap. His right hand held both the reins and the gunstock. The hours before dawn were the coldest, and Frank appreciated the warmth of Juan Carlos behind him and Tosca beneath him.

The wounded man had protested being lifted onto a horse, and now he groaned at regular intervals. Ricardo split off to deliver him to the local garrison. Dogs barked. People began to move in the streets. The horses' hooves clopped against the cobblestones but were quiet again when they reached the dirt road that led east into the countryside.

Eventually, they came to fields, groves of trees and a slow moving river. Mist rose off the water. At the end of two long rows of ash trees, Frank saw a two-story house and outbuildings. He thought he had seen pictures of houses like this—French or German, earth-toned masonry and simple, well-proportioned windows bordered with stone. Smoke drifted from a chimney, smelling of mesquite.

He saw fenced pastures and more outbuildings. He assumed the one with windows was a bunkhouse for the vaqueros. A sweetness, perhaps from a recent rain, rose from the grass around them and was mixed with the hint of something darker and dead, drifting over from the river beyond the trees.

Around at the back of the house there were two wings that, together with the main house, formed a U enclosing a courtyard. In the middle of this an ancient oak tree spread its shade over a table with two benches. A white, wide-bellied, ceramic teapot sat on the table beside a teacup with no handle.

An open outbuilding housed carriages and farm machinery. Another building, farther away, Frank supposed was an icehouse. When the horses stopped moving, Frank heard the fountain. It was closer to the main house and chiseled out of dark stone, with an artichoke-shaped bubbler at the top spilling water into two hexagonal bowls, the top one smaller, the lower one larger—all of it finished by a round, walled collecting basin at the bottom.

Frank sought the source of the water and saw a square storage tank – *tinaco* – on the roof. Beyond the roof and a little higher, a squeaking metal windmill pumped water from a well and across to the tinaco.

A Chinese man stepped forward. He was older than Frank, with streaks of gray running through his black hair, which was pulled back and fell down his back in a long braid. He had what Frank thought of as wisdom lines around his eyes, but his bare arms were strong and youthful. He greeted the señora, lifted Manuelito down and kept him in his arms, as if he had done it many times before.

Doña Mariana introduced Frank, Juan Carlos and the boy. Mr. Wu was her friend, she said. He was clearly glad to see her. She stepped forward and laid one hand on Manuelito's shoulder. The other rested matter of factly on the Chinese man's forearm. When the boy fell back toward her, wanting to be held, she laughed and said, "Manuelito, I know you're going to like him."

A pretty young Indian woman—a Tepehuana, Frank later learned—brought out a tray of glasses with blue rims and a pitcher of water. Doña Mariana introduced her as Laura and said any questions about the household could be addressed to her, as she was in charge.

They dismounted and had glasses of water while Samuel and the other vaquero led the horses away. Laura led Frank, in her lavender-scented wake, to a room with a view of the courtyard, upstairs in the main part of the house. He pulled off his boots, stood his Winchester against the night stand, drew a blanket over himself and—fully clothed—lay his head on the softest pillow he had ever felt.

He knew he had not slept very long when he opened his eyes. Sunlight still fell warm over the wooden floor. The soft white curtains moved as if breathing. He could hear the fountain. He reached out to see if the Winchester was where he had stood it.

"There's a hot bath drawn in the room to your right," said Doña Mariana, her head showing around the door. "And breakfast at the bottom of the stairs and straight ahead out onto the terrace. Just follow the smell of food." Then the door closed.

On a chair in the bathroom, he found underwear his size, a blue denim shirt and black denim trousers, all well-used. He undressed, laid his soiled clothes on the floor and sank slowly into the old narrow copper bathtub. He heard someone banging wood around; he assumed for the hot water boiler on the other side of the wall. He had just closed his eyes when there was a knock and Doña Mariana stuck her head in.

"May I take your old clothes?" she asked. "Laura will wash them later today."

"Thank you," said Frank stiffly, then sank crocodile-steady into the water with his hands over his private area, submerged from the nose down. Then she was gone. The last things he saw were her narrow waist, the long green dress she had put on falling from her hips and the white door closing behind her, leaving him to think about hips and whom they were generally attached to. For him, that was Rosa Marta.

Lying next to Rosa Marta had been like lying in warm water. There had been plenty of touching—plenty of passion. But, to be inside her, she had said, required something more formal. Frank had long since decided over the previous days that his adventure would be a short one, that Rosa Marta was the right woman for him, and that his place was with her.

When he had soaked enough, he dressed and joined the others. They sat outside, at a table on a patio in another part of the garden, in the mottled shade of an arbor heavy with small purple grapes. Frank inspected one.

"They will be ripe in another eight days," said Laura without looking at him. "And then you should eat them. Or, if you'd like, I can pick them for you."

Frank wondered about her meaning. Surely she couldn't mean he wouldn't know how to do it himself.

He sipped coffee out of a white porcelain cup with a considerable chip in it. This cup had a handle. She placed a plate of scrambled eggs with onion, tomato and chile in front of him. He looked to see if there was a chip in the plate too, but there wasn't one.

He folded back the cloth in a woven Indian basket and lifted out a thick, warm, handmade tortilla. With his fork, he laid egg on the tortilla and did his best to fold it in the way his Mexican miner friends did in Mogollón—the ends held up and sealed by the upward pressure of the thumb and little finger. Laura snorted softly, and looked away.

As Frank chewed he looked out over pastures somehow green in the middle of high desert. Polled cattle the color of sandstone— Brahman, he supposed—grazed at the far end of a pasture up close to the dark tree line that separated the pastures from the river. The animals were all soft grays and had humps on their shoulders, folds of skin hanging from their necks, and floppy black-tipped ears. He realized his hostess was talking to him. Juan Carlos was smiling. Manuelito sat looking at him, waiting to see why he wasn't responding.

"I thought you might like to know the vaqueros have groomed and fed your horse along with the others," said Doña Mariana. She pointed to the right of Frank's line of vision.

Frank leaned forward to see where she was pointing. Tosca seemed quite happy, turned out in the lush meadow where she nibbled on grass. Her chestnut coat glowed in the morning light. Two rufous-backed thrushes stalked along behind her, looking for worms, bugs, and whatever Tosca might stir up or drop. Frank thanked Doña Mariana for taking care of his horse, for the bed, the borrowed clothes, the breakfast. She said he was very welcome. She peeled a banana for Manuelito and cut it into pieces he could pick up with his fingers.

The back door opened and Mr. Wu ran toward them. He said there were riders coming. It looked like the feared rural police — *Rurales* — now "independent contractors". Frank and Juan Carlos were to go with him right now. Frank looked at Doña Mariana.

"Follow him. These are bad times. I can't explain who you are or what you're doing here."

Frank stood up. He took a final bite of his tortilla and slid the plate over in front of Manuelito. Laura stepped forward, picked up the plate again and scraped half the eggs onto Doña Mariana's plate, then put Frank's plate back in front of Manuelito.

"More convincing," said Laura, "if they're smart." Frank didn't understand.

Mr. Wu led them past the outbuildings, down a path to the icehouse, a building of thick planks and a solid sod roof. Mr. Wu slid two slabs of ice to one side. With a shovel, he cleared away the foot of sawdust and laid bare a trapdoor. He lifted a recessed ring and pulled the door open.

"In there!" he said, and Juan Carlos and Frank let themselves down into the space below the floor. Mr. Wu shut the trapdoor. They heard him shovel the sawdust. They heard him slide the ice slabs back into place. They heard him latch the icehouse door from the outside. Then there was quiet . . . and darkness. And dripping, from the melting ice. There were no windows in the icehouse, so there were no shafts of light slanting down through cracks in the floor. Nothing broke the darkness where they huddled. They found scraps of wood to sit on.

"Why are we hiding?" Frank asked.

"It's very complicated," said Juan Carlos. "She probably has all kinds of agreements with whoever controls the town. There are probably factions. Those who support the Carrancistas . . . and those who support Villa. She probably has to be discreet and give no one cause for suspicion or rumor. As soon as we can, we should move on so she is not in danger because of us."

They chatted in low voices. Juan Carlos pointed out that they should perhaps discuss Leibniz and the Enlightenment a little more, because they sat in darkness. Frank smiled. He thought he got the joke.

Then they heard the door unlatch and open. Muffled footsteps came across the floor above them. Someone stood close to right over them. Bits of wet sawdust fell on them. They heard Mr. Wu say, "There's plenty of ice if you would like a little for your use, officer." There was a grunt, then the door shut and latched. They could hear talking outside and then there was silence. They listened to the dripping for a while and then began to whisper.

"Someone must have seen us arriving early this morning. Four horses, two of them double-mounted, coming here. There's the boy, the wounded man, you and me—all leaving the train. Someone from the train . . . maybe they said something."

After a long pause, Frank asked, "Do you know if she has a husband?"

Juan Carlos said he didn't know. "There could be a jealous admirer somewhere, or someone who wants the land, or some other complication. I have no idea what's going on."

Frank thought about being in the bathtub and the green dress dropping away from her hips, her narrow waist. He could see her cutting the banana for Manuelito. He could see the white curtains in his window breathing in and out because of the soft morning wind. He thought about the pillow he had slept on.

They sat in their dark silence for what seemed a very long time until Mr. Wu returned, moved the ice aside and let them out.

"How long were we down there?" Frank asked, when they were seated again at the breakfast table under the oak in the courtyard.

"Maybe an hour," said Doña Mariana. She smiled at him . . . for the first time, Frank realized. She asked him if he would like more coffee. "Can you eat your eggs cold?" she asked. He saw his full serving had been restored. His tortilla was still there—with another very small bite taken out of it. He suspected Manuelito.

He smiled back at her but only for an instant. Unwilling to be so direct, he leaned forward again to see what Tosca was doing. The rufous-back thrushes were still there, hopping forward after Tosca, plucking something from the ground, waiting. Mr. Wu stood nearby, holding Manuelito by the hand. They were watching Tosca pull at the grass. She seemed to be enjoying the company because she did not move away.

"As I said, that's Mr. Wu," said Doña Mariana.

Juan Carlos and Frank both nodded, avoiding any questions. Frank had already forgotten the man's name and was glad for the reminder.

"I think he may have found a new grandchild," she said.

Frank noted how far Mr. Wu's braid fell down his back. Mr. Wu reached out and ran his hand over Tosca's shoulder. She shifted her head so that she was eating very close to his feet. Then she raised her head and looked at the terrace where the others ate, as if to check on Frank. Mr. Wu still had his hand on her shoulder. He too turned and smiled over at them. Then he pointed down at Manuelito and then up at Tosca's back. It was a question, and Frank nodded his head.

The mare went back to eating. Mr. Wu picked up Manuelito and placed him on the horse's back. He kept both hands on the boy. Tosca took a step now and then. The boy looked serious, apprehensive. Then he started talking with Mr. Wu. As Tosca moved, Mr. Wu moved, holding Manuelito in case he had to pull him off. It was clear the boy was in good hands . . . Tosca too.

Frank wondered if Mr. Wu was Doña Mariana's husband. Or a kind of uncle or brother.

"Mr. Wu has also hidden in an icehouse," she said. "Five years ago, when Francisco Madero's columns first came through."

"Because he supported Díaz?" Juan Carlos asked.

"No," said Doña Mariana, "because he was Chinese."

Juan Carlos nodded, as if that was explanation enough. Tosca was standing still now, with her head up, letting Mr. Wu stroke her neck. Manuelito leaned toward Mr. Wu, signaling that he wanted to get down.

"Mr. Wu is a very good man," Doña Mariana said. "You can have complete confidence in him."

"What will happen to Manuelito?" Juan Carlos asked.

"We will keep him here. Someone may have seen you take him. We will wait and see. The three riders who were just here are old Rurales from the Porfiriato. Now they are Carrancistas. They are busybodies and scoundrels. They will work for whoever is in control.

"They wanted to know about your horse, Frank. I said it was my brother's and that he would arrive separately, by train. I said the two extra men were you, Juan Carlos, a medical student returning from England, and Mr. Wu, who had walked to the station to meet us. They said they wanted to know where you were, Juan Carlos, and I said you were walking in the countryside, getting used to being in México again.

"They didn't say anything about a child. But that doesn't mean they don't know. Maybe someone who knew Manuelito's father will come looking for him. I do not think it will be his mother, since he was with his father in the war. If someone does come and I don't like the person, I won't give up the child, and he will live here just the way Mr. Wu is living here."

She looked at each of them. Frank thought she was making perfect sense.

"We should move on, so we don't make matters worse for you," said Juan Carlos.

There was a pause. "I think I need you here," she said. "We've already heard that the wounded officer from the train wants you to take care of him, instead of the not-so-sober garrison doctor. Any minute, the Rurales could bring the patient here. If that happens, I will say Manuelito is my brother's child, that he married a very young woman and they have a very young child. Something like that. It's going to get complicated, and I will need two intelligent young men to help me. At least for a while, until we can wean the wounded man away from you.

"Frank, I need you, your gentle horse and your good sense. Even your Winchester. We will keep you out of sight."

She was looking straight at him. He didn't really know about the good sense she was referring to. But without hesitation he agreed to stay. He was already well beyond the range of what he imagined his doctor had had in mind when he suggested an adventure and some fresh air. Juan Carlos, he could see, was still thinking about it all, but it seemed likely he too would stay.

CHAPTER 8

The Moon and the Tide

The wagon arrived about noon. The wounded officer lay on a bed of empty flour bags. A light film of white dust covered his face, uniform and hands. Upstairs, Frank watched from behind the curtains in his room. The officer could not stand. His head hung limp when the wagon driver and the two Rurales carried him toward the front door. Frank lay quietly on his bed and listened to the voices below, inside the house. In a while, he heard the wagon and the Rurales leave.

"He will not live," said Juan Carlos, a while later, when he stopped by Frank's room. Frank nodded, but did not take up the conversation.

When the shadows grew longer, Frank napped. Later, Doña Mariana stuck her head in. The wounded man was in a rear room on the ground floor. Frank could come down if he wished. They would be in the dining room.

He sat up and pulled on his boots. She was still watching him. When he stood up, she nodded and closed the door behind her.

Juan Carlos came into the dining room and settled into his chair as if easing down a great weight. Laura served him coffee. She asked him if would like milk.

He nodded, "*por favor.*"

She poured from a small white porcelain pitcher. The others—Mr. Wu, Manuelito, Frank and Doña Mariana—watched him take his first sip.

"Goat's milk," he said with a neutral smile.

"Is that alright?" Laura asked.

"Perfect," he said.

He looked at them all. "The infection has spread everywhere. He has a high fever. He can hardly breathe. I expect the struggle to begin tonight. Maybe you could help me, Frank. We will give him cold compresses and hold him down so he doesn't throw himself out of bed, if it comes to that. His name is Saúrez."

In silence, they ate cold slices of fried squash — *calabacita* — along with cold beans cooked with dried *chile de arbol.* Manuelito poked at the calabacita. Laura said the calabacita would make him a fast runner. Mr. Wu wondered if that was why horses ate them, when they got into the garden. Neither Juan Carlos nor Frank made any attempt to smile. The three other adults made no further attempts at lightening the mood.

Then the two younger men left the dining room. They took turns napping on a couch near the sickbed.

It was Frank's turn again just before dawn. The officer had stopped thrashing about and was lucid, watching Frank as if he were an old friend. He held Frank's hand in a tight grip.

"What will happen?" he asked.

Frank didn't know what to say. It seemed that the man was going to die. Frank had seen people in Mogollón die, from mining accidents, from influenza, from bleeding in childbirth. There were final struggles for breath or no struggle at all . . . just a slow wheezing breathing that stopped like a tide going out and not returning. Frank had never seen the ocean. In that moment he tried to imagine tides rising, then falling—pulled in and out by the moon that, in his mind, was always full.

"Your tide is going out," Frank said.

The man studied him. Frank could not read the look. He wrung out a washcloth and lay it on the man's forehead. "There's a full moon outside," he said. "The moon brings the tide back in. You could let the moon bring you back."

"That feels good," sighed the officer. "My mother did that for me when I was sick. Do you know my mother?"

Frank had already lied a few times. About the moon and about who he was generally. "Yes," he said. "She is a fine woman, someone to be proud of."

"I let her down." His voice was barely audible.

"That is not what she told me," said Frank, redampening the cloth and laying it back on the man's forehead.

Frank remembered a story his father had told him when he was a child, about a bear who saved a boy who had been swept away by a river. He began to tell the story to the man lying beside him.

"The bear slept beside the boy all night long to keep him warm. When the search party found them the next morning, the boy stood with his thin arm over the bear's shoulder and said, 'Don't shoot him. He saved my life.'

"Then they went home, and the bear would come to his open window at night sometimes and tell him news about his animal friends in the forest and then say goodnight."

Frank felt the grip loosen. The eyes still held him. The lips smiled.

"Goodnight," Frank whispered, as if he were the bear.

"Goodnight," came back the small voice. "Thank you." And his pupils began to open, and there was no more movement.

Frank sat for a while, holding the man's hand until he noticed it was beginning to cool. He felt for a pulse under the jaw, just to be sure. He pinched the nostrils together and watched to see whether the mouth would open, in an effort to breathe. Then he folded the hands across the chest and closed the eyes by smoothing down over the upper lids with thumb and forefinger. He took a lace covering off the night table and tied the top of the head and the jaw together, so the mouth would not open during the coming-rigor mortis.

He placed his hand on the man's forehead and thought a kind of prayer in which he said he was sorry for what he may or may not have done . . . for, in fact, he could not remember all that clearly. *How could he be sure*, he asked himself, *at that distance, from the ridge above, with the boy and his goats below, and an officer raising his revolver?* And now he had told the bear story to two more listeners—a Carrancista officer . . . and death.

HE WENT INTO THE LIVING ROOM — *sala* — and stood there in the early morning. He looked out the windows. He could see a horse that was not Tosca grazing fairly near the house. He stood in front of an upright piano and studied the framed photograph on top of it. There was an older couple standing together, the woman an older version of Doña Mariana, the man showing a reticent but warm smile, presumably her father. He picked up the photograph beside it. A younger Doña Mariana posed sitting in a chair in front of a standing man who had a full mustache, broad shoulders and dark kind eyes—a young face. A little boy, maybe five or six, leaned against her. The man's large hands rested on the shoulders of the woman and child. He could see how beautiful she had been, how complete her family. Not that many years ago. He felt like a thief—or a peeping Tom—peering uninvited at a private moment from another time.

The man wore a dark suit. A gold watch chain looped down from small pockets on either side of his vest. His white collar points were rounded. Below the flap of his jacket and below the gold keychain, Frank could just make out the top of a gun belt behind the boy. Doña Mariana wore a lace collar and a black dress with black buttons. Her black hair, in braids, was wrapped around her head in a manner that emphasized her long neck and her classical features.

Chapter 8: The Moon and the Tide

Frank fell quite in love with her at that moment. It was a secret he would keep to himself. As to who the boy and the man were, standing beside her, he promised himself he would never ask her.

CHAPTER 9

Vinegar and Ice

Frank walked out onto the terrace. Mr. Wu sat at the table with a pot of what Frank assumed was coffee. There were four cups and a small mug for Manuelito. The cups were white, squat and had no handles. Mr. Wu greeted him. The liquid in his cup was not coffee.

"It's green tea," he said. "It's very good for you." Frank sat and Mr. Wu poured. The tea was more yellow than green and smelled like some kind of warm wood Frank could not quite remember. It was bitter.

"How is the patient?" Mr. Wu asked.

Frank glanced at him and said, "He died about an hour ago."

"I am sorry to hear that," said Mr. Wu. "I am sorry you had to go through that."

Frank tried the tea again. This time it seemed less bitter.

"Old men drink this in China," said Mr. Wu. "The older they are, the more they drink. It keeps their bodies functioning."

Frank wondered which parts of the body it kept functioning. "How old do you have to be to drink it?" he asked.

Mr. Wu thought for a while before answering. "Maybe forty years."

That seemed like a long way away to Frank. He wondered how old Mr. Wu was. His hair had streaks of gray in it, but his hands were youthful, his forearms were rounded, and there were none of the fine hairs he had on his own arms. Frank was not going to ask.

There were Chinese miners, cooks and launderers in Mogollón and, for that matter, throughout New Mexico. He had never really focused on a Chinese person before. He could not remember if he had ever really talked to one. He knew they were clean and smart and didn't drink the way most of the other miners did.

Mr. Wu never seemed to look at him. He looked off across the fields, as if he might be waiting for someone to appear at their far edge. Frank wondered who that might be. A Chinese woman with children? Or people who did not like the Chinese and who would come after them with guns and ropes and machetes, so that they would have to flee and hide under the floors of icehouses?

Frank tried the green tea again and almost enjoyed the taste. He wondered if it would make him feel better, clear his mind, take away the headaches, the stiff joints, the difficulty in thinking things through.

"I have mercury poisoning," he said.

Mr. Wu moved his head toward him, but not all the way, at first. Then all the way.

"I know," he said.

Frank thought about that. How did he know?

"I have seen miners before," said Mr. Wu.

Frank nodded. He did not understand.

"Do you know Chinese medicine?" he asked. Frank had heard there was such a thing. He had heard they stuck needles into each other. It was hard to imagine. He wondered whether it hurt.

Mr. Wu smiled. "I know something about Chinese medicine."

"For people?" Frank asked, without wanting to be too specific.

"And horses," said Mr. Wu. "Your mare has heat in her right shoulder."

Frank knew there was a tenderness there. "How do you know these things?" Frank asked.

"I can tell you," said Mr. Wu. "If you want me to."

And over the next few days, Mr. Wu would look at Frank's eyes, his tongue, his hands, his bare chest and his bare back. He would begin treating Frank, then Tosca, with needles that he would heat first, let them cool, then stick in certain spots, tapping their heads twice with the pad of his forefinger. He would treat Frank's ears, five needles each, for mercury poisoning. He would treat Tosca for heat in her right shoulder.

JUAN CARLOS STOOD at the back door. He stretched and yawned. There was no greeting. He disappeared, then reappeared and approached them. He asked when the officer had died.

"Just before dawn," said Frank.

Doña Mariana appeared in the door and came straight toward them. She asked when the officer had died.

"Just before dawn," Frank repeated.

Juan Carlos and Doña Mariana looked at him, waiting for more.

"He was calm and held my hand," said Frank, returning their gaze. He felt hot, as if he were flushing. He looked at Mr. Wu, but Mr. Wu had no questions in his eyes. Frank felt tears form in his own. No one spoke for a while. Mr. Wu, with slow calm movements, picked up the teapot and poured Frank a little more green tea.

"You are too young to need this, but it is still good for you." Frank nodded, grateful for the intervention.

"It makes you sad," said Doña Mariana. "That's understandable." Frank took it as a question. He felt the tears returning.

"Could I have some of that, too?" Juan Carlos asked, and Mr. Wu smiled and poured tea for him. Juan Carlos drank a sip and, still holding the cup close to his lips, said, "He was hit by a sniper and should have had surgery immediately."

Doña Mariana nodded and looked out over the fields. "It is very sad." She paused for a moment and looked at Mr. Wu. "And now we have a problem."

"We can carry him to the icehouse," said Mr. Wu. "I will wrap him and put ice around him. That will give us time to think what we should do."

Laura approached with a tray. She made several trips to the kitchen. She brought scrambled eggs, beans, tortillas, salsa, slices of papaya—a bounty now available because of the railroad—and a pot of coffee to offset the presence of green tea, a drink she did not believe in.

Frank had composed himself, and now he took another stab at the way Doña Mariana and Juan Carlos held their folded, egg-filled tortillas, propping them up with their little fingers so nothing fell out. Mr. Wu took a pair of chopsticks out of his jacket pocket. He tore his tortilla into quarters, loaded each quarter with egg, added a bean or two, skipped the salsa, folded a quarter with the sticks, picked it up, and ate without loosing anything from the ends. An old tremor had returned to Frank's forearms. He folded his tortilla and held it with both hands to steady it. With each bite, salsa spurted out the ends, and beans and eggs tumbled onto his plate. Mr. Wu reached over and lay his hand on Frank's shoulder. Frank looked down and laid the tortilla on his plate. He took a deep breath, then raised his head. "I may have killed him," he said.

Everyone looked at him.

"He was in command of a mule train—probably ammunition. He went to steal goats. The boy, the goatherd, threw rocks at him. I was on a rise above them. He was about to shoot the boy with a revolver when I fired . . . from a distance. I think I hit him in the thigh. Because he grabbed himself there. He couldn't get his foot back in the stirrup."

Frank chewed a little at the bits of tortilla that still lingered in his mouth. "The boy limped," he added.

Juan Carlos had turned pale. "How do you know whether he's the same man?" Doña Mariana asked.

Frank looked at her. "I don't. But I'm afraid it might be."

"Did anyone see you?" Juan Carlos asked.

Frank thought about it.

"No, just the boy. He led me to his village. The village knows." He left out the part about the irregular soldiers and their leader.

"Then we don't have that problem," said Doña Mariana. "The only person who could testify against you is yourself. And so it is very important not to mention this to anyone. Can you promise me you won't?"

Frank nodded, but wasn't confident that he could make himself do something . . . or not do something. "We need to put him in ice," said Mr. Wu. "That's the first thing we must do."

"The first thing," said Doña Mariana, "is to prepare his body in a way that shows respect."

Frank looked at her. She looked at him.

"It's the right thing to do. And those who brought him here will interpret any lack of care as a political statement."

When they had finished eating, they went in the house. They opened windows in the bedroom, to let in the sun and morning air. They undressed the corpse and lay towels underneath him. Laura brought in a wood basin of warm water and a bar of brown soap with Savon de Marseille embossed on it. Juan Carlos bathed the wounds. The bullet, they all saw, had entered high up on his inner thigh, almost in the groin. Juan Carlos said it had probably shattered the femur. It had done terrible damage. It had come out just below his buttock—probably entering his saddle.

Laura brought vinegar as a measure against the smell of putrefaction. She added some to the bowl of warm water. The whole leg and much of the groin had turned shades of black and green. The foot was swollen and purple. Juan Carlos washed the officer from the waist down, Doña Mariana from the waist up. Frank rinsed out the rags and passed them back. Laura gazed at the corpse's penis, which lay on its side. Frank thought it looked innocent and unaware. Doña Mariana held each arm out, one at a time, holding at the wrists, and washed, Frank thought, as if they were her own. Laura brought a new bowl, this time of clay. It held more clean warm water and vinegar.

Doña Mariana washed the man's hair, in and around the ears and very carefully around the eyes. She kept the lids pressed shut as she cleaned. The washers moved quickly now, so they would finish before he stiffened. Juan Carlos stuffed cotton into the nostrils and mouth. Then they rolled him over and did his back.

Laura brought more water. Frank poured vinegar into it. As each rag came back to him, the water turned a darker amber. Juan Carlos applied more cotton, stuffing it in the last orifice. Laura looked away. They rolled him back, face up. A small amount of white showed in one eye. Frank reached out and, with a finger in each corner, pressed the lid closed.

They dressed him in a man's clean white shirt and dark suit. Frank wondered whether they had belonged to Doña Mariana's husband, the man in the photo. If that was true, he assumed the husband was not expected to return. Laura brought socks and the officer's boots.

They buttoned the shirt collar and attached a bowtie that Doña Mariana supplied. She made several attempts, fussing until she got it right—blue dots on crimson, a full soft flower of silk blooming at the man's throat. Then she brushed his hair, with care. They folded his arms across his chest, rolled him into a waterproof canvas and loaded him carefully into a wheelbarrow.

Frank pushed him toward the icehouse. Manuelito came along, holding Doña Mariana's hand. Mr. Wu fell in behind. Juan Carlos came last.

"What is that?" Manuelito asked.

"That's the officer, who died last night. We're putting him on ice," said Doña Mariana.

"He's inside that?" he asked, looking at Frank and pointing to the form wrapped in canvas.

"Yes," said Frank.

"Is he dead?" the boy asked.

"Yes," said Doña Mariana.

"And he won't wake up?"

"No, he won't," said Doña Mariana.

"Is he someone's father?"

"Maybe," said Doña Mariana. "We don't know."

Mr. Wu, Frank and Juan Carlos lay the officer on a block of ice. They shoved two more blocks up to the first one, one on either side, to cradle the body, so it wouldn't slip off. They chipped ice, with picks, and lay chunks on top of the canvas. Then they shut the thick doors behind them and walked back through the late morning sunlight, toward the house.

"Is my father on ice right now?"

"No, I'm pretty sure he's in heaven with your mother," said Doña Mariana.

Manuelito considered the information, with large brown eyes.

"But my mother is in the village," he said. "Is he with her?"

CHAPTER 10

The Same Ears

After breakfast, Mr. Wu laced his hands and gave Laura a leg up onto one of Doña Mariana's mares. With Frank's permission, Mr. Wu mounted Tosca, so he could understand more about her shoulder ailment and therefore apply the needles better. They rode on a trail up away from the Río Chuviscar, under shining poplars, with a view of the dry mountains to the west. Below them, carriages with red spokes rattled along the road beside the water. They saw heavier, mule-drawn wagons with *calabacitas, jitomates, naranjas* and green Chihuahuan *manzanas.* Once in a while they saw a complaining gasoline-powered truck with a tanbark canvas covering the back.

They dropped down, turned left onto Calle Guerrero, crossed the old green riveted iron bridge, rode until they came to the State Capitol — *Palacio de Gobierno* — at Aldama and Venus and tied their horses in the shade of the ash trees bordering Plaza Hidalgo. Mr. Wu asked the park guard to watch the horses.

He walked with Laura through a crowd of dressed-up citizens who had begun to gather in front of the palace. He asked a man what was happening.

"They're going to shoot Tomás Anaya."

"Why?" Mr. Wu asked.

"Because Villa is too weak to come and prevent it," said the man.

Mr. Wu knocked at the door that still said "Guardia Rural." The *Guardia Rural* had been disbanded two years before, when Huerta fled, trying to save his hide. These burros have the same ears, was Doña Mariana's opinion. They were unreconstructed and continued with all the old assumptions. They could pretty much do whatever they wanted.

The same two men—Jesús, the boss, and Nacho, his enforcer—who had brought the wounded Carrancista officer to the house, now sat around a desk having a late breakfast.

They stared at Mr. Wu and Laura—a Chinaman and a pretty girl. A foreigner—therefore suspicious . . . someone not above contempt—and pretty young Indian flesh, ripe for the picking.

Mr. Wu realized he had made a mistake and should have sent Laura to begin the shopping without him. "Gentlemen," he said, to a spot on the wall above the two men's heads, "we regret to have to inform you that Captain Saúrez, the man you brought to the house yesterday, died of infection early this morning."

The two policemen continued eating as if no one stood in front of them, as if no one had spoken.

"We wonder whether you have any suggestions about what we should do with him?"

Jesús lay his *gordita* down slowly, a man offended, as if he had been interrupted in prayer. Mr. Wu found him a person with little similarity to his namesake.

"Did you kill him?" Jesús asked.

Mr. Wu knew better than to respond to the question. He stood waiting, as if he too had not heard anything. A period of silence ensued, during which the Rurales alternated between chewing their food and giving them intimidating stares. Many of the looks went to the area below Laura's waist, or up higher toward the round nessof her young bosom.

Mr. Wu told them they had washed and dressed the lieutenant, and laid him on ice, and that they would be glad to bring him in as soon as they knew where he should go.

After another good two minutes of chewing and glaring, Mr. Wu nodded his head, as if acknowledging useful information, said good morning and, with a signal to Laura, turned and walked toward the door.

"Chinaman!"

Mr. Wu turned. Jesús, the *jefe* and the one with the stomach, pointed at the desk. A piece of paper lay on it. Mr. Wu approached and picked it up. It was a telegram that read: "Thank you for notification. Will arrive in two days for my brother. Sincerely, Sofía de Larousse."

Mr. Wu folded the telegram and put it in his breast pocket, watching for any objection from the breakfast desk. He turned toward the door.

"Chinaman!"

Once more, Mr. Wu turned. Jesús held a revolver at arm's length, pointing it directly at him. The man's face was blank, the pistol arm steady.

Mr. Wu nodded again, as if in agreement with something. He reached out behind him, found Laura's waist, and pushed her gently toward the exit, then he turned his back and followed her. On the other side of the glass door, he looked back and saw them still looking at him, the *jefe* still aiming the pistol at him, then lowering the gun. Neither of the men laughed, neither sneered. They just stared, *Like snakes,* he thought, *lost in some dumb consideration whether to strike or not.*

Outside, he found the same man he had talked to before. "What did he do?" Mr. Wu asked, referring to the condemned man.

"He was with Pablo López at Santa Isabel."

Mr. Wu nodded. López and two hundred men were said to have stopped a train in Santa Isabel, ordered eighteen miners to strip naked, then shot them dead, right on the railroad bed.

"At Santa Isabel," the man repeated. "His childhood friend gave him up."

Another crime, Mr. Wu thought.

The crowd fell silent. They heard the soldiers' boots as the execution squad emerged from the Palacio doors. Six men in front, six men in back, the prisoner, surprisingly young, with his hands bound behind him, limped along with his head up, nodding to people he knew.

Laura and Mr. Wu paid the park guard, mounted and guided their horses through the crowd. They could see over the spectators' heads. There were two standing iron plates, about six feet tall, each with the relief of a uniformed soldier from the early Porfirio period. They saw the prisoner, of his own accord, take a position in front of one of them.

Behind, the authorities had erected a log wall, about ten yards long that was shredded on either side of the iron plates, indicating that, much of the time, squad members fired to miss the condemned man and hit the wall instead.

Tomás Anaya's hands were now free. He was smoking a small black cigar that the squad captain had given him. Mr. Wu and Laura stopped their horses. A widespread muttering grew in the crowd and turned into angry calls against the authorities.

"Dogs! Carrancista dogs!"

The prisoner handed the cigar back to the officer in charge. Tomás cupped his hands around his mouth and, with a series of barks as if he too were a dog, thanked the crowd for its support. He raised his hands toward the sky, as if he were measuring it, then brought them down and aimed four fingers of each hand at his white shirt, indicating where to fire. He gave the orders himself, and danced back against the iron plate. A few of the bullets hit the log wall; the rest hit him, and he went down.

At the sound of the Mausers, Tosca's right front leg sagged, as if momentarily collapsing. The officer, still holding the mostly unsmoked cigar, walked quickly forward. The prisoner Tomás Anaya sat against the iron soldier form as if he were sleeping. The whole front of his shirt was red. The officer held out his revolver until it was about three feet away from Tomás' head, fired, and the prisoner toppled over, proving he had not been quite dead—only balanced just this side of death.

CHAPTER 11

Leather and Melons

Two days later, they sat outside at breakfast and discussed the threat posed by the Rurales. They all agreed with Mr. Wu that Jesús and Nacho were worse than *serpientes,* because snakes struck for a reason, and these men for none at all.

"I do not like what they did to you," Doña Mariana had said, looking at Mr. Wu.

Frank felt her statement was a pond that had no bottom. He had never seen her angry, nor had he ever seen such looks between the two of them.

Later Frank lay on the wooden table under the grape arbor, just outside the door to Mr. Wu's room. Sofía de Larousse was due, by carriage, at any moment. He was lying on his stomach, his arms dangling on either side of the padded headrest Mr. Wu had built as an extension of the table. There was a hole in the headrest for his nose and mouth, so he could breathe. He could hear everything, but see very little—only the tail of Lilus, the black cat, twitching, perhaps at the sound of an approaching stranger. Lilus rolled over, squirmed once in the dirt, looked up at him through the hole in the headrest, then leapt away to hide.

Frank listened to the voices. He wore nothing except for the small blue towel that Mr. Wu had laid across his buttocks. With his finger tips, Mr. Wu had tapped a series of thin needles into his ears, five on each side. There was no pain, and this was his fourth ear treatment in two days. Each time, before beginning, Mr. Wu would take his pulse, look at his eyes and tongue, then tap in the needles, sometimes in other places as well, to wake up the *chi,* to move the poisons, to shore up the kidneys and the liver. Twenty minutes for his front, a series of points on the top of his feet, and twenty minutes for his back and the base of his skull.

Looking down, Frank studied the spots of light that had seeped through the grapevines above him and quivered on the gravel. He reached out, felt around and picked a low-hanging grape. He put it in his mouth and crushed it. It was, alas, as Laura said, still several days this side of ripe. If he had seen Lilus, he would have flicked it toward her to inspect. He heard Mr. Wu and Doña Mariana's voices coming closer, then stopping at a slight distance, Frank thought, to preserve their privacy in conversation. Mr. Wu approached ... at least he thought it was him until he heard Doña Mariana say, "*¡Ay!,* Frank, part Adonis and part hedgehog. Sorry to interrupt, but she's here. Can I ask you to get dressed and go to your room, up the back stairs? Maybe stay there, out of sight? Until we see what we can tell her about who you are?"

Frank didn't move immediately, for decency's sake.

"Don't worry," she said, "I'm leaving."

Mr. Wu removed the needles. Frank dressed and went up the back stairs, which ascended from the kitchen. Laura watched, amused, with her forefinger vertical against her lips, as he passed through her domain. He imitated the gesture. Her eyes, he thought, said something like, "Oppose me in anything, if you dare." He smiled his apologies and took the stairs. They creaked as he climbed. He walked quietly toward his room.

The door opposite his was open, and a young woman, dressed in black, nearly as light-skinned as himself, perched on the edge of the white-tufted bedspread. She wore an ankle-length linen mourning dress and black riding shoes. Lace trim ran around the base of her long neck, her wrists, and a hand's width above the hemline. Black needlework roses climbed from waist to collarbone. Something—maybe skin—showed through in places. Frank looked away.

A round cakebox hat hid her hair, and a veil fell over her eyes but left her mouth free. In her left hand she held what looked like thirteen or so inches of bamboo the color of ebony. A hexagonal jade bowl—the width of a thumb knuckle—sat at the far end of the tube. In her right hand she held a brass spear—the length of a forefinger—with a delicate spiral handle at one end. A partially blackened button of brown substance adhered to the spear point.

She held the button over the bowl and took a long puff. The button glowed. She watched him through heavy lids. She opened her mouth. A pall of blue smoke curled up past her ears. A sweet scent hung in the air. Frank tried to place where he had smelled it before.

"I'm the widow," she said.

Frank nodded, even though he was fairly sure she was the sister.

"The maid brought me here. Is this your room?"

Frank shook his head.

"You're the medical student," she said, stating a fact.

Frank nodded his head. He wasn't sure why.

She laid the pipe and spear down on the night table. An oil lamp, also jade, also hexagonal—the size of half an inkwell—sat there burning with a small flame—presumably for relighting.

She brought up her legs and lay down on her side facing him, still wearing her black hat and veil. She watched him through the veil. He looked at her hip as it curved up against the open window, the dry hills beyond. Air moved the curtains, the barest disturbance. The long black dress showed her narrow waist, the round of her belly and her thighs. Since she's wearing boots, he couldn't have seen her "perfect ankles".

"They're looking for a tin box to put him in." She brushed back her veil to better weigh his response. "With plenty of ice, maybe he'll keep."

She took his measure, sideways, and then laid both hands under her head, in lopsided prayer. The veil dislodged and fell back into place. She closed her eyes.

"What do you think?" she sighed. "Do you think he'll keep?"

With that, she moved one leg forward, toward the edge of the bed. The shoe she presented was more a boot. Black. There were parts of it near the top that still held its shine and, below that, a coat of dust. Frank started to count the eyelets, but shifted his glance and followed the black stocking as it rose toward her calf.

"Can you take it off?" she asked.

Frank did not move. Her upper eye seemed closed. Her lower eye studied him through the veil.

"Don't be afraid," she said.

Frank reached out, halfway, then all the way. The foot moved forward a few inches, as if to help. Frank undid the knot and loosened the laces. He had never touched a woman's shoe with a woman still in it. Not even Rosa Marta's. The leather was familiar, similar to Tosca's tack, but thinner, so it was not so different from uncinching a small saddle.

He tried to pull off the boot by holding the toe and pulling down on the heel, but it would not come. She twisted her ankle a bit, as if to give him an idea.

Frank raised her dress a little, as he would if it were a veil. It was easier to think of her as a small horse, so he gripped her hock through the stocking and worked the boot until it was off in his hand.

He placed the boot on the floor and continued holding the hock in his left hand like a farrier who was not quite done. The stocking was compressed from the pressure of the boot. She wriggled her foot a little to wake him from his trance.

A smell of powder, leather and foot, all mingled with something like melon, hung in the air. He lay the foot down on the bed, relieved to be at the end of the task.

She drew it back and, with a swish, brought the other one forward.

"Halfway there," she said. She had pushed back the veil again, and both brown eyes were round with attention. "How old are you?" she asked.

For a moment, Frank could not remember. It seemed more like a question about distance. Like, how far have you come? He searched the open window for the answer. It also seemed like a question of how long he would live. He looked back at her. She wriggled the second boot. Frank took it off. She retracted both feet and folded them back under her skirts, like chicks under a brood hen.

"Hold my hand for a moment," she said, and brought her lower hand out from under her chin. Frank, who thought he recognized sadness, obliged and took her hand.

"Two hands," she said.

Frank held the small white hand in both of his. His hands were tanned. Blond hairs grew on the backs of them. Holding her hand was like holding a bird.

"Sit down," she said, squirming her hips back a bit, and then lying still. The veil had slipped back down to the bridge of her nose. The curtains lifted out into the room and then billowed back out into the open air. She twitched a few times. Her mouth went slack, her lower lip crooked. Saliva pooled at the corner of her mouth. It slid in a thread onto the bedspread, where it made a spot of wet between two tufts. Her ribcage rose and fell. Her hand fluttered. He lay the hand up near the veil and got up carefully. A crocheted, yellowed, wool foot-warmer lay on the only chair in the room. He spread it over her hips and legs. He blew out the jade lamp. He put his hand on the latch, to pull the door shut behind him.

"Thank you," she said, as if from some place deep under the earth.

CHAPTER 12

Gudgeons and Pintles

Frank entered his room. He felt sleepy—from the needles, perhaps—and thought he might snooze. He stood for a moment at his window, looking down. He saw Mr. Wu and Doña Mariana, in a white riding dress and light green denim jacket, standing in front of the French doors that led into his quarters. He watched Mr. Wu open the door, then turn and take Doña Mariana's hand. Frank stepped back a little, just as she began to glance up at his window. He saw her look around, then follow Mr. Wu into his room. The door closed. Mr. Wu pulled his white curtains across the door windows. Had he been closer, Frank thought, he might have heard the bolt slide home.

He had held the widow's—or was it the sister's—ankle in his hand, but he had thought about Doña Mariana's ankle, her riding boots and her long green dress from before. Now she had taken Mr. Wu's hand and gone into his room with him. He felt tightness in his chest.

They had all eaten together, consulted one another. She had asked him, Frank, to stay and help. Mr. Wu was treating both him and Tosca. Doña Mariana had seen him in the tub and on the needle table. It had never occurred to him that they, she and Mr. Wu, could turn their attentions toward each other.

Frank imagined Doña Mariana sitting on a white tufted bedcover and Mr. Wu taking off her riding boots. He saw him combing her hair with a carved Cantonese comb with long smooth teeth—the kind he had seen his father give his mother—that moved the blood in the scalp and produced dreamy smiles while she took off her stockings.

At this very moment, Mr. Wu was probably washing her feet in water he had warmed ahead of time, anticipating her arrival . . . then rubbing them with an oil that smelled of melon. Then he, someone, or Frank himself, moved his strong warm hands upward past her calves, moving the oil higher.

Then she was sitting on Mr. Wu's bed with one leg dangled over the other, bouncing her upper leg, smiling. Then she was lying on her stomach, like an Adonis—which he assumed meant someone partially or totally naked—with needles in her back and ears—which, after ten minutes, he would remove so she could turn over—smiling, with her hair splayed out and her arms reaching up to hold him.

Frank drank a glass of water. It didn't help. He felt dizzy and sat down on the bed. He took off his own boots and lay down. The drowsiness from Mr. Wu's needles had disappeared, and his thoughts raced.

He got up, pulled his boots back on. He went down the back stairs, out the back door and walked past Mr. Wu's French doors without looking at them. He walked toward the pasture. Laura was pushing Manuelito in the rope swing hanging from one of the ash trees near the front of the house. Laura waved. There was no challenge in it. The boy waved quickly, so as not to fall. Ahead of him, Tosca raised her head, whinnied a greeting and trotted toward him like a dog that knows she's going for a walk. Her sore shoulder moved smoothly. There was no limp. He walked ahead of her. She followed. She snuffed and breathed in his ear as they went.

He opened the gate to the next field, swinging it on its old oak hinges—like a ship's rudder on its pintles and gudgeons. The mare walked through. He closed the gate behind them. He gripped Tosca's mane with his left hand and flopped his stomach over her back. Tosca stood obligingly still. He swung a leg over and rode bareback across the field toward the far gate. He opened and closed this gate from a mounted position, jockeying Tosca with knee pressure and heel taps.

When he reached the river, he took the trail east. In a grove of cottonwoods he met Juan Carlos coming from the opposite direction on Doña Mariana's brindle gelding.

"No saddle?" Juan Carlos asked.

"Good to see you," said Frank, who was glad to have a friend.

They leaned toward each other and shook hands. Juan Carlos turned the gelding, and they rode beside the Chuviscar. The afternoon was warm, the river smelled of mud and just a hint of something else—muskrat shit maybe, rotting vegetation, dead things that drifted unseen. The cottonwoods stirred, their leaves dark green and light green. Frank felt the prickly heat of Tosca's belly, her coarse hair, her reassuring smell of horse.

CHAPTER 13

The Roan and Mr. Wu

Mariana remembered the day with absolute clarity. Two years ago. She had gone, alone, out to the stable to check on the roan mare. The horizon to the east, just above the blue peaks, glowed from the still hidden sun. She saw her breath in the air. Frozen grass had crunched under her boots. The mare had greeted her when she entered the stall, swinging her head to find the apple she smelled in Mariana's hand and giving a low nicker in gratitude.

Mariana had fed her the apple, mushy from winter storage, one quarter at a time, palm up, and had felt the tickling of the rubbery lips against her hand. The mare had thick winter hair, brown flaked with gray and white and was barrel-bellied, ready to burst, but still in no discomfort.

———

AND SHE REMEMBERED two years before that—now four in all—she, Alfredo and their son Iván, just turned six, had come out to the stable together to attend the roan's mother. They had brought apples that time too.

It had been the middle of the night on Three Kings Eve. They had heard the mare calling, grunting, thumping the wood floor of the stall. They had gotten up and dressed, waking the boy, cutting the apples. In the kitchen Alfredo had rested his hand for a moment on her bottom. His way of saying, at this crazy hour in the middle of the night, "You are my love."

Iván had carried the bag with two green apples cut into quarters. Alfredo had pumped water into a bucket and carried it into the stall. He had left the door open while he went for a pitchfork of hay. Mariana had curried the mare, while Iván fed it apples, careful to keep his small hands away from the animal's teeth.

She remembered her husband and son, the two great loves of her life. Alfredo's smile, crooked, turned up at the corners with equal measures of mischief and adoration.

She remembered that the next day, with the foal already sucking on her mother, Alfredo and Iván had driven to town. Four carriages had been crossing the bridge at the same time, and the bridge gave way. All had fallen ten yards into the Chuviscar. Horses, carriages, beams, girders, iron, wood and the two most important things in her life—all entangled and held down against the mud, until life was gone.

In a day, the wreckage had shifted and the bodies—most of them—had risen to the surface. When the river dropped, boys had found five more bodies in a back eddy, floating in circles. They had dragged the bodies up onto the sand, just far enough to put an end to their drifting. One—a man—had been too heavy, and so they had taken the lead rope from a neighbor's burro and tethered the man's leg to a branch, until Mariana, hand over her mouth, had come to claim him as her Alfredo.

His body had rolled first this way, then that way, only a few feet away from their beached son, who, unlike his father, had lain face up and peaceful on a pillow of sand.

She hadn't slept. She hadn't eaten. That night, on her orders, the vaqueros had put the boy in the cypress box with his father. Alfredo on his back. The boy facedown on his father's chest with his father's arms around him. They had wrapped rocks—the equivalent of Iván's weight—in the boy's blankets and arranged them in the smaller casket. No one else knew. She had watched them lower the caskets—four men, two ropes for Alfredo's, two men, two ropes for the smaller one. The impossibility of it all. The numbness that would not leave her body. Her resentment of the new foal whenever she saw it—a resentment that had taken months to dissolve.

SHE REMEMBERED when, after two years had passed, with the predawn glow along the horizon, another foal was coming. She had put on a thick wool jacket and gone out to the shed. She had pumped water. The pump handle had been cold. She had set the bucket down in front of the roan and stroked the animal's neck, giving reassurance and warming her hands.

When the mare lowered her head to drink, Mariana had dropped down on one knee, put her ear against the horse's neck and listened to the gurgle of the cold water passing through the animal's throat.

When she had opened her eyes, her ear still pressed against the great warm neck, a man was standing absolutely still in the dark corner of the shed, looking at her, unmoving, as if remaining still would prevent her from seeing him.

For some reason, she had not been frightened. He had watched her. She had brought her head away from the roan's neck and stood up. The man was small, Asian, probably Chinese. He had not had a coat. Strands of straw had clung to his shirt. Most likely, he had been sleeping with hay pulled over him. He had gotten up, but had had nowhere to go when she'd come in.

He had seen her feed the roan the apples. He had seen her listen to the horse drink. He had seen her remember Alfredo and Iván. She had thought she saw alarm in his eyes, but also something else—perhaps an apology, or even respect for the privacy of her thoughts.

"I do not mean to scare you," he had said. He did not move. He slowly wrapped his arms around himself. "I will go," he had said.

The roan had thumped the floor and begun to turn in circles. Then she had lowered herself onto the floor and lay on her side. Mariana had pulled a horse blanket off a hook and held it in her arms.

She had looked at the intruder. "Are you from Torreón?" she had asked.

He had nodded.

She had walked toward him. "Put this around your shoulders," she had said.

He had taken the blanket.

"I know what happened in Torreón. You are safe here," she had said.

The mare had groaned, flapped her tail and strained.

Mariana had gotten another blanket and laid it over the roan. The mare had groaned again and rolled her eyes. Her rump and neck glistened with sweat. "Is this her first time?" the man had asked.

"Yes," said Mariana and went behind the mare to look.

"She's tight," he had said. Mariana had said she knew, and they would just have to wait.

Rays of sun passed through openings between the boards on the east side of the stable. They had been able to see the mare's distended vulva.

"We just have to wait," Mariana had repeated.

The man had been older than she was. She had not been sure by how much, but she felt no threat. He had walked to the mare's head, knelt and stroked her neck. Then he had held his hands against her, the fingertips of one hand between her eyes, the others on her chest, equidistant between the front legs. He had spoken softly in his native tongue.

Mariana's first impulse had been to tell him to step away, that she knew what she was doing.

The mare gave a great sigh, and the man continued to press. He was well-meaning, she had thought, but she knew about these things. The mare would do it in her own time.

She had glanced at the mare's vulva. The roan had pressed and said something in a low whinny. The bluish membrane had appeared. She had been able to see the small front hooves pressing from the inside of the sack. Then came the shape of the head.

A ribbon of sunlight lay across the event. Mariana had knelt and eased the narrow shoulders forward, always waiting for the mare to press, supporting the foal's head with her upper arms. The man had spoken encouragement in his soft language and pressed on the same spots. The roan had given one more push, and the foal had slipped out into Mariana's arms. With a sob, she had fallen back into a sitting position with the warm foal in her lap. She had wept as she peeled the blue membrane back away from its face, greeting the newborn with a confusion of words, laughing and crying at the same time, praising the mare she had wronged, asking her forgiveness.

The man had gotten up from his knees and taken the horse blanket from his shoulders and wrapped it around Mariana's, whose whole frame was shaking. And then he had knelt beside her. "A beautiful foal," he had said, touching its forehead. "And a good beginning."

CHAPTER 14

Herbs and Arrows

On his eighth birthday, Wu Lian went to his father and asked for a bow and arrows. His father was a small but successful businessman on Fuxing Road, in the French Concession of Shanghai. He sold medical supplies to health practitioners throughout the smoky city.

"I will not give you a bow and arrows," said his father, partially hidden behind the smoke from his clay pipe. Lian's mother looked up from her sewing. Lian dropped his head until his chin rested on his collarbone. He held his breath. He did these things so he would not show the disappointment that gripped his heart.

His father sucked on his pipe. Two billows of smoke rose around his head. Lian's mother remained motionless. Lian had nowhere to go. He was too old to go to his mother and lean his head against her neck.

"I will not give you a bow," his father said again. "But I will send you to the Japanese master Shinsaku Hogan to learn to shoot an arrow with unfailing accuracy . . . "

He paused and took another puff.

Lian's head, still bowed, was now also heavy with thought.

" . . . if you agree to study how to repair and comfort the human body with the same unfailing accuracy."

Lian's mother's hands relaxed on her sewing. Lian lifted his head. His father's eyes were the color of ebony. Lian saw the question in them. He saw the invitation.

"You will learn to shoot many bows and different types of arrows. At the same time, you will learn medicine, mathematics, history and culture. That is my wish for you. What do you say?"

Lian had heard his father close deals with doctors and healers. "What do you say?" he said in such cases, too. He heard a sound from his mother, a quick inhalation, a gasp, an urging that he answer the question.

Lian was thinking, at that very moment, he would like to learn to smoke a clay pipe as well.

"I would like that, father," he said.

Wu Lian did in fact study with the master Shinsaku Hogan, until it was rare for him to miss even the smallest target. He learned all the names and uses of all the herbs used in Chinese medicine. He learned all the acupuncture points of the human body, young and old, and by the age of twenty-five, he could bring healing and comfort to his clients, and, with time, to many types of animals as well.

In 1894 the Japanese occupied Shanghai. Korea was ceded to the Emperor of Japan. Taxes rose and food was scarce. Disease ran rampant throughout the city. Wu Lian's mother, father and Master Shinsaku Hogan all died in the same year.

Wu Lian heard about an organization in México and the United States called Bao Huang Hui that helped Chinese immigrate. He believed that México would be more open to Chinese medicine than the United States, so he chose México and boarded a ship bound for Mazatlán.

He had practiced in Torreón for some years when, on 15 May 1911, Madero's revolutionary forces swept into town and, together with a rabble of the poor and dispossessed, began killing as many of the 700 Chinese residents as they could find. The following night, Wu Lian, along with other specially-trained men carrying women and children who were too terrified to walk, glided beside walls and ran along creek beds to a remote icehouse on the outskirts of town, where, under the thick floor and the ice, they hid silent and in darkness until they could be evacuated to a protected train bound for San Antonio. The bodies of 303 murdered Chinese were burned in a vacant lot, without a single person in attendance, except for those stoking the fire.

CHAPTER 15

Monarchs and Mules

Frank and Juan Carlos were riding side by side, letting the river flow, the trees rustle, the horses think. Two boys in shorts, seven-year-olds perhaps, crossed their path, following a creek up and to the left, away from the river. They were going swimming, and yes it was a good place. The riders turned their mounts after the boys. The animals grazed along the way, taking a leaf here, a leaf there, from the over-lacing oaks. One of the boys reminded Frank of his baby brother. For a moment, he saw Philip's face looking up from his coffin. But there was too much life in these boys, and the image faded.

They climbed about a mile. The boys skipped along ahead, periodically glancing back, proud to be leading adult riders to a special place. Long-needled pines with rust-colored elephant skin guarded the pool. It was hot country, but the feeder stream was fresh. Frank assumed it bubbled out of a mine farther uphill. It snaked down through a clearing and then fell into the pool. The smell of pine flowed through the forest, and the ground shimmered with mottled light. Orange butterflies settled and took off, fluttering over the green spot where the waterfall splashed onto the bank.

Juan Carlos dismounted, passed his reins over the gelding's head and looped them around a pine limb that was low enough to let the horse graze. He loosened the girth. Then he stripped, lay his clothes on a flat rock and crossed the grass to the pool.

Frank slid off Tosca's bare back. He gave her a couple of distracted, loving pats on the rump and let her graze freely beside the pool. It had not occurred to him that Juan Carlos would take his clothes off. This caused him a few moments of hesitation. He considered Juan Carlos' well-shaped calves, the backs of his thighs and buttocks. He decided they had roughly the same sized manhood, but Juan Carlos was a little softer in the midriff. He kicked off his boots and stripped. Frank stepped into the water. His own skin was much paler. The boys, two tadpoles near the shore, studied his whiteness and his manly things.

Frank stepped deeper. He squatted, cupped his hands and brought water to his face. It smelled clean. He thought of baptisms he had seen. The boys played near the bank. The butterflies took moisture from the grass by the waterfall. He had never seen such a concentration—clouds of butterflies rising up and swirling their orange against the sky's blue. Frank admired painters and wanted to be one if this was what they saw.

He and Juan Carlos swam with dignified breaststrokes around the pool. Frank suspected the boys could not swim. He kept an eye on them. The gelding and Tosca thumped their hooves. They blew out now and then like whales, sounds Frank had only read about. They grazed without looking up.

He lowered his feet and stood. He brought water up to his face again. It seemed to help him consider the women in the house. Laura's flirtation, her dark intelligent eyes. Sofía de Larousse's black stockings and her pout. Doña Mariana's green dress falling from her hips, and her white dress disappearing through Mr. Wu's door.

He put his head underwater. He rose and wiped water from his eyes. The boys murmured and floated sticks. Frank was sure that, without the sound of the waterfall, he would hear the wings of the butterflies.

Juan Carlos swam up to him and planted his feet.

"It's quiet, isn't it?" he said.

Frank nodded, his chin partially submerged.

"You're going south, they're going north," he said quietly, moving his arms in a stationary breaststroke. "And neither of you knows why," he grinned.

Frank thought about it, cupped more water, rose a little higher and washed his face again. He needed a bit more time to consider the remark.

Tosca's head came up, and her ears pointed back down the trail. They heard the click of hooves on stones, some in the stream, more on land, and the clank of metal. The gelding whinnied. The boys rose up to get out of the water. Frank rose to the top of his pubic hair. There was still time to grab his clothes or just mount without them and disappear into the forest. He turned his head. Two men stood on the grassy rise above the waterfall, carbines raised, stocks against their shoulders, aiming at them. Frank sank back into the water. He had a vision: the butterflies turning gray, the pool red.

The armed men had come around behind them, Apache irregulars maybe, or Tarahumaras or Yaquis. Men who can run without making a sound, without tiring. Their eyes flicked from the pool to the forest looking for danger. They lowered their rifles. Four riders crashed into the opening from the downhill side. Others came behind them but, fifty feet off, crossed to the other side of the stream. Men and horses flowed uphill, curious eyes on the swimmers, an 8mm Hotchkiss machine gun strapped to a mule followed by two more mules with wooden ammunition boxes—then even more mules with more machine guns and more ammunition. Red dust rose up into the afternoon light.

The four riders dismounted, faces glistening with sweat. Three of them lay right down on their backs to rest. The fourth one sailed his wide-brimmed hat to the ground, unbuckled his below-the-knee chaps, lifted his two bandoliers over his head, lowered his gun belt with two guns to the ground, let them flop, undressed and tiptoed toward the pool; stopped, pissed, studied the gelding and Tosca, jiggled himself and then entered the pool.

He smiled at the boys. "I used to swim here when I was your age," he said. Then he gestured with his head toward Frank and Juan Carlos. "They with you?"

"Yes," they said. They had brought them to swim with them.

The man nodded, then did his own dignified breaststrokes toward Juan Carlos and Frank. He stopped in front of Frank. He wiped water from his face. Water dripped from his mustache. His body was pale below his neck. When the man was still outside the pool, Frank had noted that his manhood was larger than his own, and that he had testicles like a goat.

"Those are monarchs," said the man.

"Heading north," said Juan Carlos.

"No, heading south," said the man, with a tone of authority. "To Angangueo, for the winter."

He turned toward Frank. "I recognize your horse, gringo," he said, smiling. "You appear to be heading south too." Then he swiveled his head, as if he were checking on the boys.

"Can you swim?" he barked over at them.

"Almost," said one of them, proud to be addressed by an important man.

The important man turned to Juan Carlos. "Are you the doctor?" Frank wondered how he knew that. Juan Carlos nodded as if his neck were frozen.

The man turned toward Frank again. "Gringo, do you know who I am this time?"

Frank had the impulse to sink out of sight. He cupped water and brought it to his face again. "I know you are interested in nature, that you don't want the boys to drown, and that you like music. Otherwise, I'm sorry, but I don't know who you are."

The important man nodded ever so slightly, in disbelief.

"Listen," he said. "Tomorrow we are attacking Chihuahua to show the Carrancista bastards and the Americans we are still a force. It has to be a surprise. I can either shoot you, or keep you under guard for a day. You choose."

Juan Carlos could not speak.

Frank hesitated. He thought back to their previous encounter. He meant it as a more reasonable way of being together when he said slowly, "If you have the piano, I could play again."

The Jefe sputtered, "*¡Ay!, qué pendejo,*" and turned away.

He swam over to the boys. He said something to them. The boys looked over at Juan Carlos and Frank, then back at the Jefe, as if weighing authority against allegiance. They whispered with each other, their backs to the adults. Then they turned around.

"You're staying?" the taller one called over to them.

Juan Carlos nodded and raised a dripping hand in farewell.

Juan Carlos and Frank swam over to the Jefe. "What did you tell them?" Frank asked him.

"I told them they were good kids and if they told anyone about us I would come and hang their parents."

He stared at them. Then he turned and climbed out, showing them his swinging goat balls, now chilled and reduced. He ordered them to get dressed and mount. The other three riders stirred and got up. To the largest of the three, a tall man with a bushy mustache, the leader said, "We're taking them with us. Shoot them if they make a run for it."

"Why not shoot them right now?" asked the tall man. The Jefe glared at him, the same way he had glared at Juan Carlos and Frank.

"And the boys," said the tall man, without fear.

"This is a special place," said the Jefe. "Do as I tell you." He let his gaze linger on the man. "Besides," he said, "we've got a doctor and a musician."

CHAPTER 16

Maggots

Juan Carlos and Frank dressed quickly and mounted. The six of them rode past the Indian scouts at the top of the grassy slope, above the pool.

Frank saw that each of the scouts wore a long knife at his side. The lighter skinned one wore a silver necklace with a Christian cross. The Jefe signaled to them to follow. Without turning his head, he shouted back to the scouts, "Cut them if they ever try to escape."

The path narrowed. First boulders, then cliffs rose on either side of them. Then they were near the top, in a field surrounded by pines. At least one horse was tied to each tree, sometimes two. Their saddles sat on the ground close by. Riders spread open tarps and tossed batches of alfalfa on them, so the horses would waste nothing. As the horses ate, bits of the hay fell back onto the canvas. Frank wondered where an on-the-move attack troop had found alfalfa. He wondered if they would come for Doña Mariana's alfalfa, or had already. He wondered how many times the Jefe had threatened to hang people if they reported the appropriation.

He estimated there were a thousand men in and around the clearing. Men carried canvas water buckets back from the stream for the horses and themselves. They had stood their old Mausers in tripods, using the swivel clip toward the muzzle to join them. They sat in small groups talking. The light began to fade. Women entered the clearing carrying bundles of food and bedding. Junior officers moved about the camp, warning that there could be no fires. That each man should clean his rifle, rub down his horse, then lie down to rest. And anyone who went more than seven meters beyond the clearing would be shot. Almost no one complied—except with the seven meter rule.

In all, there were three Hotchkiss guns; they and the extra ammunition remained on the mules. Everyone would mount and leave in two hours.

Men got up and moved among the horses, finding a place to squat. They made watery sounds or strained against uncooperative bowels. With no breeze to carry it away, the smell of shit hung over the camp. The soldiers scraped themselves with pine needles, bits of newspaper, cold tortillas or dirt. Then they walked to the stream and washed their hands, upstream from others who had flopped down to drink—until guards were posted, warning them to wash downstream.

The Jefe led them to a grassy spot upstream, beyond the water drinkers, where a young woman lay on blankets, with two women in attendance. Three Mausers lay beside them, along with bandoliers of ammunition with gaps here and there, like missing teeth. A little apart, the riders dismounted.

"She's dying," said the Jefe. "If you fix her, I let you live." He threw them one of his stares. "If you don't, I will shoot you."

Frank took off his canvas hat. "With all due respect," he said, remembering how his father could politely admonish someone, "I wish you could ask us for something without threatening to kill us."

Juan Carlos slowly shook his head. The Jefe looked at Frank. He too shook his head, but with more force. He held his vertical finger close to Frank's nose, his eyes glazed and bulging.

"*Cuidado,*" – "Take care," – he said. His breath had an edge, like cooked beans that had turned. "I swear, I have chickens smarter than you."

"Ah, Pablito," said a small voice, from the blankets.

The Jefe lowered his hand. He relaxed his forefinger. Then, with more head shaking, he spun around, inserted his left boot into the left stirrup—his horse knew to start forward—skipped once on his right leg, swung up, and man and horse cantered away, sending bits of dirt and grass back at Frank and Juan Carlos.

At first the women would not say where the wound was. Juan Carlos knelt down beside the patient.

"I'm a doctor," he said.

"You're a man," said the older of the two women who stood in attendance and appeared to be in charge. She had long gray braids and a box jaw. Her khaki skirt, with slits on each side, was stained from many hours on the trail. The exposed skin on her legs carried a patina of dust. At the end of her braids, she wore short strings of blue beads. Frank wondered how much of her blood was indigenous, and from what group. Maybe Apache.

She stood on the other side of the patient, boots planted far apart, leaning slightly forward, as if she were ready to leap at Juan Carlos.

He looked up at her. He said they had to choose between modesty and saving her life.

She said he was only worried about his own life. The Leader would finish him off if he didn't save her. She had heard him say it.

Juan Carlos said that was true, he didn't want to get shot, but the young woman still needed attention.

She pointed at Frank.

"He'll move," said Juan Carlos, and he indicated a spot up beyond the victim's head. Both the position and blankets would block his view.

Frank got up and sat cross-legged in the position assigned to him. The other woman and Frank exchanged a look. She was as young as the victim, and pretty. Her teeth were white, and her breath—had she been that close to him?—was sweet, like freshly mown grass. She had a gap between her front teeth and eyes that crinkled in amusement. *Perhaps,* Frank thought, *in appreciation of the struggle between Gray Braids and Juan Carlos.*

Juan Carlos asked, "*¿Con permiso?*" and slowly pulled away the blanket, which was black with the victim's blood. The cloth stuck to the wound at the top of her right thigh.

He said he needed hot water.

"No fires, "said Gray Braids.

"What is your name?" Juan Carlos asked.

"Berta," she said.

He said she should make a small Indian fire, just enough to heat water. There would be almost no smoke. He took out his jackknife and held it up. "To sterilize this," he said.

Berta scowled at him. "That's a bad idea, going into her. And no Indian fire," she snorted.

"She'll die," said Juan Carlos. "And then we're fucked too."

"There, you see!" said Gray Braids, pointing at him, "just what I said."

Frank had never heard Juan Carlos swear before. He and Gap Tooth exchanged a look.

The victim rolled her head toward Juan Carlos. In little more than a whisper, she said, "Pee on me."

Juan Carlos looked down at her, frowning.

"What's your name?" Berta asked.

"Juan Carlos," he said, without looking away from the patient.

"Well, Juan Carlos, they didn't teach you everything, did they. You say we need to get the cloth away from her. Warm pee will do that. And so, with your permission, I am going to take your place."

Then she stepped over him, hardly giving him time to get out of the way. She turned around, raised her skirt and squatted. She sighed, gushed, and almost immediately the smell of warm urine overwhelmed the lingering smell of shitting men. Frank watched, his eyes wide. He had never heard, let alone seen, a woman pee before. Berta stood, dropped her dress, and stepped away. "Well, did you see that, gringo?" she said, without even looking at him.

Frank wanted to glance over at Gap Tooth, but decided against it. He could feel her eyes on him.

Juan Carlos waited a few minutes, then returned to his place and slowly lifted away the urine-soaked blanket. The patient wore a soiled, white dress. Someone had already pulled the skirt part and underwear down around her boots. The bullet hole was below the groin, three or four centimeters to the inside of the femoral artery and nerve. She had been lucky. But her entire groin was dark with blood. He leaned his head down to smell. The young woman's hand found his forehead and held him back in protest. He felt fever in the hand. The odor was rank and troubling. There was shit and old urine, and, behind that, the smell of infection.

With the blanket pulled away, the wound oozed new blood. Juan Carlos pressed it with three fingers until it stopped. Berta and the other young woman, whose name was Merce, rolled the patient onto her side. Juan Carlos leaned his head closer to hers.

"What's your name?" he asked.

"Antonia," she whispered.

"How do you feel?" he asked.

"Smelly," she said, "and sick." Juan Carlos lay his hand on her upper arm and gave her a reassuring squeeze. Fighters passed by, and, on orders from Berta, Frank held up the blanket so they could not see Antonio's naked backside. He did not look down at the patient.

"There's infection," Juan Carlos said, in a low voice, to Berta. "If we had lime leaves, we could make a tea to put on the wound."

"We can't build fires, " said Berta.

"Then she will die," said Juan Carlos.

Berta said something to Merce, who jumped up and left.

Juan Carlos ripped away part of his own shirttail and made bandages, one for the front of the thigh and one for the back. Berta handed him a small piece of dark soap. Juan Carlos frowned at her.

"I forgot I had it," she said.

Merce came back, carrying a basket with a lid. She put it down in front of Juan Carlos. She raised the lid, as if presenting a treat. Juan Carlos and Frank leaned forward and saw a goat's head swarming with maggots. They reeled back from the smell.

"We put them in wounds," said Berta.

"That's crazy," said Juan Carlos. He remembered vaguely reading about maggots and infection, but he couldn't remember what. His head ached, and his hands began to tremble.

"Then she will die," said Berta.

"This is crazy," he said, in almost a sob. He tried to remember about maggots.

"They eat the infection," said Berta. Juan Carlos rubbed his eyes. Yes, he had heard something about this. Maggots did something, or had something, that sterilized wounds.

"We should rinse them first in the stream," he said, "In cloth, quickly, so we don't hurt them, then put them at either end of the wound."

Berta nodded approvingly. She and Merce plucked the worms from the rotting goat head. Merce dumped out the contents of a small cloth bag: her comb, two pairs of earrings, the stub of a pencil, some hair clips, and a cartridge, which Frank estimated to be 38 caliber.

Berta and Merce put the maggots in the bag. He went with them to the stream and watched as they lowered the bag into the water and gently swirled the maggots. Like a dog that wants to be included, he followed them back to the patient. He saw the two Indian trackers watching him from the tree line. He still didn't know whether they were Tarahumara, Apache or some other group. What he thought was that they might very well have come after him with their knives if he had crossed the stream.

"They claim they're Comanches," said Berta, dropping back, her voice lowered. "They're mixed-bloods, escaped from your missionaries—Jesus Christ, long knives and peyote. A bad combination. Stay away from them. Do you understand me, gringo?" She strode ahead without waiting for an answer.

Frank looked up again at the tree line. The two Long Knives were still watching him.

Juan Carlos pressed the maggots slowly into the wound's entry and exit holes. At each touch, Antonia gasped. Then he applied the bandages and bound them against her thigh with a long piece of cloth, this time ripped from Frank's shirttail.

At that moment, the Jefe rode back over and dismounted. Berta drew the blanket over Antonia's nakedness. Antonia pushed the blanket away so her man could see her.

"*¡Ay!, chica,*" said Berta and covered her again with the blanket.

"Did you fix her?" said the Jefe, to no one in particular.

"The bullet missed the femoral artery," said Juan Carlos. "The wound is infected. We cleaned maggots and put them in the wounds. She's bandaged. She needs peace and quiet."

"Fucking stupid of you," said the Leader, but he was nodding his head.

"It's what saved your ass after Guerrero, my General," said Berta, staring straight at him.

The Jefe glared at her with a dark smile, then at Juan Carlos and finally at Frank.

"What are you smirking at, you dumb gringo?"

He spun around, found his stirrup, and mounted again. He wheeled the horse so he could look at them all. "Keep her alive," he said, pointing at Juan Carlos. He pointed at Frank. "Stay out of my way, gringo!"

Then he wheeled his horse again and sank his spurs into its flanks. The horse exploded forward. Dirt flew back, and the General galloped toward the far end of the encampment.

CHAPTER 17

Duty

Sofía de Larousse had hired a wagon and three men to retrieve the tin casket from the icehouse and deliver it to the train station. An uneasiness reigned in the house when she came to say her goodbyes. The medical student—who she thought looked like someone from north of the border—and his friend had not returned, two hours after nightfall.

At the station, the casket remained in the wagon. She paid the carriers and the driver. The driver unhitched the wagon and took the mule away. He would return in the morning for the wagon. Potential thieves would think it belonged to the stationmaster. She shouldn't worry about it.

Sofía de Larousse argued with the stationmaster, the new guardian of the wagon. "Why aren't you loading the coffin?" she complained, with slow words.

He said it was, as she knew, September 15. The 12 A.M. south-bound train had arrived but would not leave until some time after the celebration of *El Grito*—"*Viva México, Viva México, Viva México*"—at midnight.

Drunken revelers liked to shoot at locomotives to see what would happen with all the steam. Besides, the coffin's hinges were defective, they didn't close all the way and the contents had begun to smell, and he could not allow the box on the train unless it was placed in the last cattle or horse car. In any case, it could not be loaded until just before they left, to avoid troubling the animals, a condition that would change when the train was underway and air was passing through the slatted sides of the cattle car.

Sofía de Larousse accepted these conditions, mostly because she had smoked a pipe of the brown paste just before setting out. She was content to sit in the light of a kerosene street lamp, on an iron bench with her back to the station, watching the fireworks over the city and the people celebrating the Cry of Independence. She enjoyed seeing a group of running soldiers who wore the uniform her husband had worn and therefore were Carrancistas like him and adherents to constitutional order. She was happy to see several of these young uniformed soldiers position themselves behind the wagon with the casket.

She sat quietly, glad that she was fulfilling her duty as a wife and bringing him home, when something exploded on the wall just behind her and shards of brick rained down over her black hat and dress. She continued to sit quietly, crowned in brick, as bullets splintered the spokes on the hired wagon and made metal sounds when they punctured the casket.

A young Carrancista dropped his Mauser, fell face forward and lay still. A liquid poured in a thin stream from the tin casket—as if her husband were peeing one more time—and joined the thicker liquid already forming around the fallen boy. Two young soldiers, handsome in their uniforms, crouched behind the wagon and looked over at her, whimpering. Dirty-looking irregulars with rifles approached the wagon, firing as they came. They walked around it, then right up to the two Carrancista boys, and shot them at point blank range.

CHAPTER 18

The Widow's Abduction

The General's forces had formed into columns. One would attack the Palacio. Another would overrun the penitentiary, where they hoped to free José Inés Salazar and other Orozquistas—former enemies, but now possible allies against Carranza. Frank and Juan Carlos were something between prisoners and conscripts. The General had taken Juan Carlos—as his personal physician—to the government palace. They had separated Frank from Juan Carlos. They needed a doctor, but they didn't need Frank.

The scouts who had outflanked them at the swimming hole followed Frank and, like him, were part of a third column approaching the barracks. The time had passed when he could warn someone about the attack. Nevertheless, the scouts stayed close to him. They admired Tosca. He had seen it in their eyes. When the moment was right, they would put a bullet in his back. It would happen near the beginning of the attack, along with the first shots fired. They would attach the lead rope first, as if they were guarding him more closely. He could see it all with unusual clarity. His situation was not good; he rode bareback, did not have his rifle and the two scouts rode close behind him.

The column came to a stop. The riders sat on their mounts, not speaking. The lieutenants in front were conferring, waiting for something. There were crowds up ahead. He saw the station to his left. A train stood on the platform. He heard the first shots, the beginning of fireworks, and church bells beginning to ring. His group moved their horses forward slowly and without formation, their rifles still in their scabbards as if they were just revelers coming to join the festivities.

"What are the bells for?" Frank asked a horseman beside him.

"*La Independencia*," said the man. "It starts at midnight."

Other riders joined them. Men dressed for Sunday carried a child or two in front and a wife behind. All kinds of people were on their way to the central plaza. The crowd was aglow with *pulque* and shouts of *Libertad.* Men fired rusty pistols in the air, and a sympathetic population heard, then took up, a new cry that seemed to have started very close to him: *¡Viva Pancho Villa!*

One of his watchers came up on his left, with a coiled lead rope in his right hand. Tosca stood still. Frank held out his left hand, as if to assume the task of attaching the lead rope to Tosca's neck. He was cooperating with his captors. A rocket burst overhead and became a ball of bright sparks that twinkled and faded. Frank pointed up at it, an old trick his father had taught him to use on other boys. The Indian, no fool, kept his eyes on Frank. His grip on the rope did not loosen.

The column up ahead leapt forward. This was the moment. Frank rolled to his left, unencumbered by stirrups. With both hands, he grabbed the scout's right foot at the ankle, pulled it out of its stirrup, and held on to it as he fell, so that he, Frank, would land on his feet and be stable while the Indian, with his leg forced around and over his horse's rump, would crash to the ground.

Except that the scout, all in one motion, kicked off the remaining stirrup, drew his rifle from its scabbard and swung it, along with the coiled lead rope, in the same arc his body was twisting, and landed the barrel near the top of Frank's head—a glancing blow, cushioned by his old canvas hat, but enough to knock Frank to the ground. The Indian, on his feet, staggered backward with the momentum of his dismount and rifle swing. In that moment, the charge began, and the horses sprang forward as a single mass.

From instinct, the scout chose to remain with his horse rather than deal with Frank. He caught his horse's saddle horn with his left hand, leapt and rolled at the same time, and landed behind the saddle, still holding the rifle and lead rope. Pinned among other riders so he could not turn and go back, he pulled himself forward onto the saddle and hurtled away with the rest of the column—including Tosca, who was also forced forward.

Frank got up and ran toward the train. There was shooting everywhere. He crawled under the nearest passenger car and held very still. A streetlamp cast a shadow under the car, but Frank wondered whether it was enough to hide him.

He had barely finished considering his cover when a rider approached the car he was under, exactly where he was crouching. No one dismounted. Still, he felt trapped. If the scout jumped off his horse, that would be the end of it. He would come at Frank with a rifle or knife, and there would be no stopping him.

Frank worked his fingers into in the rail bed, loosening the rock. The gravel smelled of old wastes, straight from railway toilets. He had three pieces of gravel in each hand. If he threw them hard enough and from close enough, he might hit an eye. The horse pawed with a front hoof, as if it wanted the rider to either dismount or move on. Frank lowered his head a little. He could see all the way up to the horse's chest, but he saw no stirrups and boots. And then there was a soft, low whinny, and Frank realized that it was Tosca, that she had broken loose and was riderless.

Frank came out from under the car. He flopped up on Tosca, swung up, and rode around the end of the train. A woman dressed in black, with a hat and veil, sat on a bench in front of the station, with a travel satchel beside her. There was a wagon, with its tongue lying on the ground. Three uniformed soldiers lay dead beside it.

There was a coffin-sized box on the wagon, and Frank realized the woman on the bench, with the black hat and veil, must be the widow of Captain Suárez. He approached and slid off Tosca.

Sofía de Larousse had imagined herself standing up and shouting, *Stop that right now!* as the irregulars slaughtered the Carrancista boys right in front of her. But she had not moved, and the killers had gone on. Then she felt a hand on her wrist.

"Take my arm," said Frank.

She took his arm. With the other hand he grabbed her travel satchel. If they ran, they could be a target, so they walked. She was dressed like a widow. He would be her escort. They were waiting for the train's departure.

Carrancista soldiers streamed by everywhere. He wondered whether the attackers had underestimated the resistance. The widow tried to pull away. She hissed. He clamped her hand tighter. She dislodged it. He caught it. She pulled, like a dog clenching the end of a rope. Abruptly, she went limp. He held her up. He pushed her up the steps and into the car he had hidden under. He opened the door on the other side. They waited.

Tosca came around the end of the train, saw them and cantered up. Frank pulled on her mane and clucked her into position, close to the steps. He pressed the widow over Tosca's back, held her by the back of her thighs, and pushed her farther into balance. Then, still holding the satchel, he sprang forward, onto the widow's back and buttocks. He heard her wheeze. Still on top of her, he swung a leg over Tosca and sat up.

The widow gasped for the wind he had knocked out of her. He gave her a few slaps between the shoulder blades. Then he pulled her up and worked her dress up and lifted her right leg over until she sat straddling Tosca in front of him. He held her arms straight up until she regained her breath. He put the satchel on her lap and told her to hold it.

"You bastard," she gasped.

He touched Tosca with his heels. With his arms around the widow's waist, they moved along beside the cars. Faces peered out at them in fear, people trapped, taking cover in the train. The widow's stomach muscles were rigid with anger.

They came to the end of the last car. Frank rumbled a "whoa," and Tosca stopped. They listened. The shooting seemed to have moved toward the penitentiary. He could hear what he assumed was the major battle near the Palacio in the other direction. They moved forward a little and stopped again, looking back at the station.

Two small men—who, judging from their clothes were clearly impoverished—worked the casket out of the back of the wagon. They carried it a little to one side and then, releasing the rings at the same time, let it drop. They stepped back, swiping at the front of their trousers where something had splashed them.

The widow breathed in sharply and brought her right fist down hard on Frank's thigh.

"*¡Tranquila!*" he growled, and suppressed an impulse to throw her off the horse.

The body collectors heaved and pushed. The corpses of the three young Carrancistas were young and healthy, weighed something and sagged in the middle when taken by the hands and feet. Using their knees and shoulders, the men finally got the corpses into the wagon. Then they ran around to the tongue, picked it up and pulled the wagon off toward the barracks, where they would receive a few centavos for the dead delivered with their uniforms—once the shooting stopped.

No one shot at Frank and the widow. He kicked Tosca into a canter, then thought better of it and slowed to a walk. They passed the station. They passed the leaking casket. Sofía de Larousse let out a sob, but muffled it with her hand when she caught the smell of her husband. Frank too held his breath. He turned his head right and left, looking for danger. He felt the widow's shoulders slump.

"My husband," she said.

"I know," said Frank. "I'm sorry."

He held his left arm around her stomach. His right hand lay on her right thigh, steadying her. He felt her lean back against him.

They followed the corpse collectors for a block, then turned off and entered narrow streets, where people offered them *pulque*. There was much nervous excitement, whether for the uprising or the Independence celebration, Frank couldn't tell. People looked up and down the street and sat on the edge of their wooden chairs, so they could leap up and hide if soldiers appeared. They ate tamales, piled husks in the middle of the table and drank punch.

Home fireworks—of diminished power—fizzled overhead. Men held rockets at dangerous slants, so that they ricocheted off house walls instead of lifting into the night sky. Children held firecrackers in their hands for too long. A boy threw one under a table and got shouted at. Tosca flinched right and left. People smiled at them and held up glasses. They called out "*¡Viva México!*" but mostly "*¡Viva Pancho Villa!*" followed by bursts of laughter.

"Mexicans!" Sofía de Larousse muttered, but Frank had no idea what she meant.

Now in the dark streets away from the shooting, she relaxed against him again. Her head bobbed forward, her weight grew heavier, and Frank realized the woman he had abducted—the woman who had covered his own escape—was fast asleep. So he moved his hands farther forward, to hold the travel satchel as well.

They left the river and turned toward the house. There was no moon at all. He saw Tosca's ears go forward, then he heard "Frank," something above a whisper, and saw one of Doña Mariana's vaqueros ride out of the trees and fall in beside him.

"Where is the doctor?" Samuel asked.

"With the group that's attacking the Palacio."

There was a pause. "Voluntary?" ask Samuel.

"No," said Frank.

Another pause. "Are you alright?" Samuel asked.

"I think so," said Frank. His head hurt from the rifle blow, and the question made him want to cry.

"What about her?"

"She's okay."

At the house, Mr. Wu stepped out from the shadows. He went over to Tosca and lay his hand on Frank's knee, and asked him if he was alright. Frank nodded. Was she okay? Yes. He kept his hand on Frank. He turned to the vaqueros. They reported the attack was faltering—information gotten from passers-by on the road along the river—as there were too many Carrancistas.

Juan Carlos was at the Palacio. Mr. Wu said it would not be good if Juan Carlos were captured. They would come to the house, looking for everyone in it. Samuel said he would go back into the city to see what was happening. They paused to listen. They could hear the shooting in the distance. Then there was a detonation that rattled the front door window.

"Shelling the Palacio," said Samuel. "With a three-inch gun, I think."

Mr. Wu touched Tosca under the jaw and told her to follow him over to the steps. She appeared to move even before Frank had tapped his heels. Mr. Wu reached up for the widow.

"Her name is Sofía," said Mr. Wu.

Up to that point, Frank had not given a thought to whether or not she had a first name. Mr. Wu brought her down slowly and stood her against himself. Frank dismounted. One of the vaqueros clipped a lead rope around Tosca's neck and led her toward the stables.

"You take her," said Mr. Wu. Frank leaned down and laid her over his shoulder and stood up. He climbed the back stairs as quietly as he could, moving slowly to keep from bumping her head, allowing space for the satchel.

He laid Sofía on her bed. He lit a candle and untied her shoes. This time, though her eyes were open, she did not help. He took off her shoes and unpinned her hat. He undid the buttons on her jacket, to relieve the pressure on her chest and stomach. Like uncinching a horse. He lifted her head and put a pillow under it. He lifted it again to clear away the tresses of her partially braided hair. Then he blew out the candle, wet his fingers and pinched out the still glowing wick. He left her door open.

In his own room he lit the candle on his night table. He took off his boots and hat and lay on top of the bed with his Winchester beside him, its muzzle pointing toward the foot of the bed. Through the open window, he could hear the crackle of rifle fire. Each time a cannon boomed, the window rattled.

He thought about Antonia and the maggots. He thought about Berta, who would be watching over her. He worried that the Carrancistas would find them. He worried about Juan Carlos, who might be trapped in the Palacio, looking after the wounded and dying. Would being a doctor save him from the wrath of the Carrancistas? Would they bother to question him? Would they believe him if he said he was a doctor? That he had been a prisoner? He saw the tin casket that was leaking Sofía's husband. He saw the scout, balanced like an acrobat, swinging the rifle at him.

He must have drifted off. The door opened and Sofía entered, all white without her clothes. She climbed onto the bed, on the side nearest the window. Frank turned toward her. To make more room for her, he lifted the Winchester and put it on his other side.

She lay facing him, on her side, with her eyes open. She took his hand and laid it across her bottom. She did not release his hand. She watched him. He smelled melon mixed with pipe.

"Are you alright?" he asked.

She nodded. She closed her eyes. Frank waited a while, then tried to remove his hand. She breathed deeply, but would not release it. He reached out with his other arm and pinched out the candle. The night breeze moved the curtains. The rifle fire seemed intense. He heard Tosca's low fluting whinny inquiring after him from the stable.

The door opened again and Doña Mariana entered. She came up to the bed. She looked down at Frank's hand, on Sofía's hip. Frank looked up at her. She had on a robe. It was partially open, and Frank thought, if there had been a little more light, he would have seen her breasts. She put her hand on his forehead and lingered there, as if checking a child for fever.

"Are you alright?" she asked.

He nodded. She took her hand away.

"We were very worried about you. Now we're worried about Juan Carlos."

She leaned forward and kissed him on the forehead. She straightened, leaned forward again and kissed him lightly on the lips, then left the room, closing the door softly behind her.

Frank turned a little, like a dog, trying a few times to find the right position between Sofía and the Winchester. He dislodged his hand from her grip. He eased onto his back and looked up at the ceiling. Doña Mariana's visit had robbed him of the sleep he so much needed. But he also found some comfort in thinking about it. She might have had something on under the robe. He tried to remember what exactly he'd seen. He did not know what to make of women coming to him and touching him. In Mogollón, in New Mexico, Rosa Marta seemed to touch him without touching him. He tried to see Rosa Marta leaning over him at night, the top of her robe open, the candle burning—when he realized Doña Mariana was leaning over him and shaking him awake.

"Get up, Frank! We've found Juan Carlos." She cupped his face with both hands. "Get up! We have to go right now."

CHAPTER 19

Escape

The group that had attacked the Palacio had long since stopped guarding Juan Carlos. There was no need to. At first, they had fired from the windows, scattering the Carrancistas who ventured into the light of the streetlamps. But then someone had snuffed out the streetlamps, and they had become the targets themselves. It was easy for the Carrancistas to fire at the dark outlines of the palace windows. On the inside, it had become impossible to approach the windows or even be in a room with windows.

Juan Carlos was working in an interior room away from the windows that faced the square. At least twenty men and boys were lying there in their own blood, asking for help, weeping—bellowing like cows being slaughtered.

He had been kneeling in blood. Blood soaked his shirt and his lap. He could feel it soaking into his shoes and felt the stickiness between his toes. Dust choked him. His throat was as dry as a snake's shed skin. Every so often a bullet would find its way into the room, its force mostly spent but lethal enough still to make the wounded scream and cover their heads.

Juan Carlos worked up against the wall where there was the most protection. Men inched toward him, begging for help. He pushed them away with his feet, sliding them easily back over the film of congealing blood. He tried to keep clear a space for himself and the person he was working on. There was no medicine. There were no bandages. He used a bayonet to cut parts of clothing that were still dry and bound wounds any way he could.

Then the cannon fire began. The building shook with each impact, a shower of debris and dust blasted through the door. In the flash of the detonation, Juan Carlos saw a young man clawing at his shoe. He braced himself against the wall and kicked at the figure, so it would back away.

The rifle fire dropped off for a while. They were letting the cannon do its work. Its shots had become more frequent. He suspected they had unlimbered two cannons now and that they were aiming for the windows, to lessen the damage to the outside of the grand old building and to do maximum damage to the people inside the building.

The man he was working on had a stomach wound. Juan Carlos could feel it, not see it, the man's tunic open, the warm intestines lying over the top of his stomach. By feel, he tucked them back into their cavity. He didn't have a piece of cloth long enough to tie around the stomach. Even if he had had one, he could not imagine how he would get it under and around the man's body.

In a lull—through the ringing in his ears—Juan Carlos heard the man say, "I'm going to die, aren't I?"

It caught him off guard because the man had given words to it all, and Juan Carlos felt fear stir like an animal in his chest. The young soldier at his feet was back and clawing his way up his leg, pulling himself closer. Other men huddled against the wall, crowding against Juan Carlos. He held his hands over the exposed intestines of his patient. In the flashes, he saw men covered in dust, like penitents in ash, watching him, as if at any moment he would lead them away to safety.

Someone grabbed him by the back of the neck and from very close said, "Get up, we're leaving."

He tried to stand but stumbled over his own patient, who screamed. A hand steadied him and pulled him toward the door. They waited to one side for a moment. The next blast hit some other part of the building. His patient sobbed, "Take me with you."

"Let's go," said the voice. The man took Juan Carlos by the hand and led him deeper inside the building, then toward fresh air and the barest glow of night. There was a group of men and horses, just outside a gate. The man handed him some reins.

"I think this is your horse," he said. And then, "Get on!"

Hands held his slippery left shoe in the stirrup, other hands lifted his buttocks and supported him until he could swing his leg over.

"Ready?" asked the man.

"Ready," said several other voices.

Juan Carlos listened for the command. He sensed the gelding's tenseness. "May God have mercy on us both," he mouthed. At that moment, the man who had come to fetch him said, "Go!" and they broke forward in a serious gallop, choosing one side or the other of their horse's neck for cover.

His rescuer—a man he did not know—rode the horse in front of him. The first shot came from close by and knocked the man back over his saddle. His arms dangled. His whole body began to slump to the left. Bullets exploded against the houses on either side of them. The rescuer's horse slowed. Juan Carlos, alongside him now, grabbed him by his bandolier and pulled him toward himself. He leaned to counteract the weight of the rider's body. Both horses slowed. Riders swept by on either side. Horses went down. Men fell. His rescuer's boots would not come out of the stirrups. A third rider, seeing the problem, struck the backside of the rescuer's horse with his rifle. The animal bolted forward, pulling the stirrups with it and releasing the wounded man. The third rider grabbed him by the gun belt and heaved him farther across Juan Carlos' saddle and saddle horn, and then raced on ahead.

Juan Carlos knew they had fallen behind. The plaster dust that covered them made them good targets. He decided to take his chances. He slowed the gelding to a walk and took a side street toward the river. The shots grew weaker behind him. He was unarmed, though no one could see that. He carried a man across his saddle horn. He could be a civilian recovering a body—except for the wounded man's bandoliers. They were clearly fighters who had been in battle. The man lay on the bandoliers' buckles. There was no way to get rid of the bandoliers. He rode toward the Chuviscar. He felt for a pulse and thought he felt one. But he also felt a new, warm stickiness in his crotch from the blood on his saddle.

He rode one street back from the river. The houses were farther apart. He dismounted and rearranged the body so that it lay across the bowl of the saddle. He walked the horse until they reached trees and bushes. He followed cattle trails a little away from the road. He stopped and listened. Then he crossed the road and led the horse down to the river. Pulling the man off the saddle, holding him under the arms, he laid him down on a patch of grass beside the water, at a clump of willows that blocked the view from the road.

Wading into the river and sitting down in the water, he washed the plaster dust from his face, hands, neck and then his clothes. Loosening his belt, he unbuttoned his trousers and reached in to wash away the blood, both old and fresh, from around his penis and testicles, holding them for a while, with both hands. Juan Carlos had almost forgotten about the man who had saved him from certain slaughter; saved him so he could be caressed and held by a woman he loved.

He crawled through the water quietly, stood up, hitched up his trousers and stepped onto the grass. He knelt and felt under the rescuer's jaw. There was no pulse, so he searched the man and found a folded leather pouch, with a few papers. He would look at them by daylight. If there was a surviving wife or relative, he would find them and tell them what had happened.

He stayed beside the body and listened to the night sounds: crickets, the sound of Doña Mariana's gelding eating close by, ripping at river grass, gently snuffing. The shooting had almost stopped, but the cannons were quiet. There were only individual rifle shots. In his mind's eye, he could see the Carrancistas moving from room to room in the Palacio, executing survivors—the men he had tried to help.

He cried for a while, then got up and remounted. His body felt cool and clean. He needed to be very careful, so he decided to dismount and lead the gelding through the willows, putting distance between himself and war and hangings and firing squads.

Because he needed to get back to the house, he mounted again and guided the gelding through the river and across a field to find the road that led east.

Then someone shouted a command from the road ahead of him, so he turned the gelding to the right, into the field and back toward the river. The soft meadow would be quieter, plus they couldn't really see him. But then there was a single rifle shot—somebody making a calculated guess. It was a grazing shot, maybe more, because the gelding cried out and danced its rear legs forward unnaturally, then broke into a panicked gallop across the field.

Juan Carlos hung on, making reassuring sounds, patting the animal's shoulder, trying to take off some of the pace. The gelding slowed a little, his stride still even, in spite of the wound. Juan Carlos had a plan. He could not predict the surface of a field. He would cross the river again. He would get away from war.

Men shouted. There were shots, closely spaced. Someone had set up one of the new machine guns. The bullets slapped against the trees ahead of him. He swung left. Maybe he had misjudged the gun's position. He swung farther left. But that was wrong, too.

The flashes and roar were in front of him. The gelding increased its speed. He should have turned right. He had made a mistake. They had checkmated him. His neck went numb. I am a doctor, he thought. It is the fear and sadness. He could feel the gelding collapse beneath him, then there was a blow and a great weight upon him.

As his breath was leaving, *he saw the young woman in the white dress smiling and saying, "Juan Carlos, get up. Juan Carlos, get up!" over and over, and Juan Carlos replied, "You mean, play another game? Is that what you mean?"*

CHAPTER 20

Where the Purépechas Sit

You will pardon me, patient reader, if I invoke here the "grandson privilege" and at this point refer back to the steamer trunk with its resident rats and disordered documents.

There was a letter that is key to this portion of the narrative amid that muddle. My own father's careful Palmer Style appears penciled on the envelope and explains that in the fall of 1918, Frank returned to Chihuahua with Rosa Marta. On this visit, he wrote a letter to the local priest, a Father Ibarra, about a matter that had been troubling him for some time.

The letter is in English, I suppose because in the end he needed his own language to express the full range of his thinking on matters that were both philosophical and theological.

Father Ibarra, it appears, considered the letter something of a historical document and felt it belonged with my family. How it got into my father's hands and then into the trunk before it was sealed behind the barn wall, I do not know.

The final sentence of my father's penciled note reads, "For other generations to follow," but I knew nothing about the events described in the letter. In the most generous interpretation—to absolve my father of the sin of omission, family censorship or New England reticence—I believe I understand how history "for future generations" can nevertheless slip our minds until the stories nearly die, and how in this case it was only because of my older sister, her crowbar and her screeching eight penny nails that they did not.

Dear Father Ibarra,

I have heard that you were transferred back to Mexico City, but I know that you are still important to Doña Mariana. You stood by her when she lost her husband and child. You stood by her through the troubles. For that I respect you profoundly.

It has taken a great deal of time to recover from the little adventure my doctor told me to take.

You will remember the event that I refer to. I am sorry we did not have more conversation when we were walking back from the Chuviscar. It was a spot where Juan Carlos had gone to swim a few times, by himself and with great pleasure.

You were shaken that we burned him, that we included the horse in the fire and that we had placed him on top of the horse. When our paths split, you said that you were sorry that he had not been more religious—that it would have been easier for his soul.

By the time you had arrived, sweeping the sandbar with the hem of your robe as you came, the fire was no longer at its hottest. What you saw was, I agree, not an everyday occurrence. But what do you do with one dead horse, let alone with the thousand cut down by Obregón's machine guns in the second battle of Celaya?

First, the hungry come, with knives, stepping over the human corpses, going straight to horses, hoping for a cut of rump at the risk of being shot for looting. The troops on both sides pull back. The dogs come and wrench their heads right and left, ripping at the soft spots, beginning at the horse's anus or at the genitals on humans. The living throw rocks, and the dogs and vultures shift to a different pile of flesh. The hungry cut as much as they can carry. The smell is not yet offensive enough to keep them away. There are not enough men and shovels to bury so much death. There are not enough teams to haul the horses to gullies. Later, with so much rot, the legs pull off when drag ropes are attached. Everything pulses green and yellow with flies and maggots, and then the people walk away. The dogs rip and tear and gorge until they vomit. The buzzards finish, leaving a field of bones to whiten in the sun.

We had only one horse, and we did not intend to wait for the dogs or the buzzards, let alone the people. The same Carrancista Hotchkiss that killed the horse also killed Juan Carlos. Samuel and Mr. Wu found him by chance after the soldiers had withdrawn. One bullet had passed through his throat, about where the top shirt button would be. By lantern, we saw the gaping wound. Four bullets had struck the horse, all frontal entries—in the chest, shoulder, rib cage and top rear leg—as if it had been the main target. Horse and rider had plunged to the ground. They lay tangled when we found them, with the horse on top, covering my friend, except for one arm and one twisted leg.

Samuel returned to the house, along with Mr. Wu, to tell Doña Mariana what had happened and to protect the house. There was no telling who would come through looking for supplies, horses or women. Doña Mariana knew an ox driver, and he arrived within an hour. We dragged the horse off of Juan Carlos. I had long since determined there was no pulse in the exposed leg or wrist, so it did not pain me quite so much when his body came along with the gelding before being peeled back away by a protruding rock.

We could not lift Juan Carlos up onto Tosca, perhaps because we were in too much shock, too much grief, so we tied a rope to his ankle and, with Tosca pulling, joined the procession, taking our place behind the oxen and the horse's carcass.

The horse's body smoothed the ground before us, but dragging Juan Carlos was still unbearable, so we stopped and rigged him under the arms to keep his head and hair out of the dirt and leaves. That didn't work because the rope slipped up and dragged him by the head. I tried tying him by the right wrist and left foot, the rope looped over Tosca's saddle horn. But then he bumped along on one hipbone, so we stopped again. With my hand I could feel that we had worn through his trousers and were tearing away at his flesh.

We threw the rope over a cottonwood limb. I lifted him and Doña Mariana took up the slack, holding each gain by wrapping the rope around the trunk of the tree. We finally had him more or less standing, and then I maneuvered Tosca until we could lift his lower half up over the saddle.

Samuel and Mr. Wu had found them at about three o'clock, and it was about four by the time we had the horse at the sandbar on the Chuviscar, where Juan Carlos liked to swim. The ox team assembled driftwood, in some cases whole logs. We piled brush around the horse. Without discussion, we pushed and dragged Juan Carlos up onto the horse's belly. Then we piled more brush, dragged more logs, and still more brush, until the pyre covered them both.

I had long since stopped crying. I do not remember when I started or when I stopped. But when we lit the fire, I think all my accumulated sadness rose to the surface, and I wailed with such terrifying sounds that my hostess put her arms around me from behind and held me for as long as it took for the fire to burn hot—and me to grow calm.

The ox driver, a man with a long history with the earth, had laid heavy stones on top of Juan Carlos. I protested, but he said it would give us comfort in what was about to happen. In the furnace we had created, the horse's upper legs took on an angle, and Juan Carlos' arms cast off the stones anyway and rose up as if he were lying in bed reading and holding a book over his chest—in the end, without hands.

Dawn was coming and the stars faded. A river of sparks curved up and away. The fire crackled and spit. River stones exploded from the heat. A slight breeze came up. The three of us stood upwind, so we would not have to smell the roasting horse, which was acceptable, or Juan Carlos, which was foreign and troubling.

That is when you arrived, Father Ibarra. Doña Mariana and I were standing with an arm around each other's waist. The ox driver had given us his sympathies and gone home, perhaps to give us privacy. He would not accept any pay. He said we would have done the same thing for him. He had hugged each of us, in spite of the class differences, in spite of my being from the north.

You, on the other hand, seemed filled with indignation and disapproval. I do not know how you learned what was happening. Perhaps a devout member of your church had seen us dragging a horse and a man, or building a fire, or placing a man on the horse so that the fire would take them both. I do not know what the nature of the alert was, but I imagine you came to express your concern for the treatment of a human soul.

Doña Mariana finally asked you to stop speaking and do whatever you needed to do to put your own soul at peace. Only then did you perform what I suppose you consider the final blessing for someone too late for the last rites. You spoke Latin and brought your gold cross up and held it against the fire. Then you went behind us and stood for a long time, saying nothing. By then the fire had fallen in on itself and formed a mound of glowing coals with a blanket of gray on the outside, which the wind periodically fanned and turned momentarily golden.

That was when the ox driver returned, on foot, without his lumbering oxen, carrying a shovel and a frayed knapsack. You went and sat on a rock farther back from the river, reluctant, I suppose, to fully end your supervision of the various souls at risk.

While the ox driver waited patiently, Doña Mariana and I took off our boots and socks and waded, fully clothed, into the river, the deep part, and settled into it and murmured a few words, but mainly watched the sunrise and the poplars emerge green and alive on the opposite bank. When we got out, we took turns and threw shovelfuls of ashes and coals out into the river. Clouds of ash rose with each toss. The coals hissed. I made a pile of larger horse bones, and I suppose a few from Juan Carlos, for dogs to take at their will. But everything else went into the river, including the ends of logs, which I rolled into the water, until they floated and departed downstream, steaming like ships setting out to sea.

You had moved even further back from the river, as if the distance would insulate you from any participation. I remember feeling touched by your concern when I assumed that some part of it was for our spiritual well-being. The ox driver again hugged us, took his shovel and left. Before he left, he took two oranges out of his old knapsack and said we should eat them and enjoy them as our breakfast.

On the way home, you fell in with us but were not able to speak. Doña Mariana had saved two sections of her orange for you, which you took and immediately ate with something between hunger and gratitude. You seemed happier, I thought, perhaps because your spiritual storm had passed, and you could be included again in our world.

That was when you said what you said. I think you meant well—that you were sorry that Juan Carlos had not been granted a more religious treatment and that it would have been easier for his soul if he had been.

On this point, I have to tell you something I knew about him. Something he told me in one of our conversations.

In one of Lake Pátzcuaro's small villages, he had come out of a *cantina* on a late fall afternoon and had seen a Purépecha family sitting on a recently dead horse beside the road. The mother and father sat between the front and back legs with their two children on their laps, their legs dangling over the curve of the animal's belly.

Juan Carlos had sipped enough of the local *mezcal* to allow himself a brief theological discussion. He asked them whether when something so large and so Mexican died, didn't it use up a big share of death, more than it needed for itself, so that there was then less of it, less death, for the people sitting on the horse, and life was better and stronger for the living?

The Purépechas, he said, looked at him as a curiosity in his own right. Perhaps it was because he had implied they were Mexican, when in fact they were Purépecha. The woman had glinting jet-black hair, the color of the great-tailed grackles that wake us up too early, commenting on everything and keeping us honest, even when they are not. Her hair fell forward over her bosom in two braids, with a blue silk ribbon woven into the tresses and joining both braids at the bottom. She was very pretty, and Juan Carlos tried not to look at her.

He had read about the Socratic method, and so he thought he'd use questions, gentle of course, to explore their thinking. Why were they sitting on the horse? Did they believe that some of its strength and goodness passed on to them? The wife started to speak, but her husband made a sound, as if warning a dog away from something that might be poisonous. He said they were sitting on the horse because it was there. Juan Carlos asked, was it because its life was still recent? The husband said his wife believed their children were healthy because of God's protection. But he himself believed it was because he had married her young and strong . . . and pretty, he said, and he laid his hand on her knee and gave Juan Carlos a warning look. She nodded, embarrassed, and did not look at Juan Carlos again. Then the family got up and walked up a path that led away from the road and up into the mountains.

Juan Carlos, it appeared, had asked enough questions to inspire scientific inquiry in himself. And so he, too, climbed up on the horse's belly and stayed there, considering things until long after a great moon came up over the lake and the last bit of warmth had left the horse. He noticed that many dogs had gathered around him, sitting patiently, some lying down, looking at him, at each other, at anything other than what was really on their minds. For a while, he considered whether it was his duty to continue sitting on the horse, to protect it from what was going to come. But he saw the practical problems, so he got up and walked carefully through a break in the ring.

Father, you and I have both seen México's stray dogs. When a horse falls in war or peace, no service comes to whisk it away. Instead, dogs strip the corpses clean, hollowing out the belly first—their faces red with blood—and carrying off every last bone, including the head, in as little as two days.

If you will permit, each time I see this, I think I may be looking at some kind of communion. I ask myself whether some goodness doesn't transfer from the horses to the dogs—even though they continue to be neglected, kicked and despised.

I have read, Father, that horses served us for thousands of years before Christ was born. Unless ruined by humans, they are known for their spirit, for their service and for their loyalty. They have the power to make us better than we are, and that is why I think the Purépechas were sitting on the horse in Juan Carlos' story.

I write this letter because I want you to understand that Juan Carlos, even with the help of a little *mezcal,* could not have asked the question he asked the Purépechas if he had not believed in some sort of redemption. Both Doña Mariana and I had heard the story and we thought we knew where he should lie. We burned Juan Carlos on top of his horse because we believed that the death of his horse would make it easier for his soul, not harder, and that companionship in fire would see them through whatever journey lay ahead of them.

We will be heading north soon. I do not need a reply to this letter, Father Ibarra. I simply wanted you to know my thoughts on the matter of who is sufficiently spiritual, and who is not. I am sorry we did not get to know each other better. I think you meant well. As I know we did.

Respectfully Yours,
Frank Holloway,
from the house in Chihuahua

There was a companion piece to Frank's letter. A handwritten page on lined paper attached by paperclip. The pencil writing—as noted by my father—is in my grandfather's hand. It reads as follows:

For those of you who one day might be interested in where you come from, I add this note. Fifteen days after writing Father Ibarra, a different priest stood at Doña Mariana's front door, holding a beautiful brindle mare. He asked for me and handed me an envelope when I came out. The letter was from Father Ibarra, thanking me for my letter and commenting that the mare was one of the finest animals he had even seen and that it was a gift from him to me, " . . . for all the travels that might lie ahead, for both of you." By which I'm quite sure he meant the horse and me and our souls. And that when times were better I should visit him in Mexico City at the address in the letter, and that we would have grand conversations.

I thanked the young priest, who then walked away. Since I already had had the finest mare in the world, Tosca—and because I no longer did—I gave the horse to Mr. Wu, who I knew would know how to love her and care for her as he did for Doña Mariana.

Doña Mariana wrote me every year on my birthday until she died in 1936, at the age of 60. Mr. Wu died a year later, apparently unable to live without her. I do not know what happened to the brindle mare . . . or to Father Ibarra.

CHAPTER 21

Departure

When Father Ibarra said goodbye, Frank and Doña Mariana mounted and crossed through the poplar and ash trees, crossed the road and entered a path that was seldom used. They watched the house from deep shadow. They saw Mr. Wu come outside with Manuelito and Laura. Manuelito sat with his cup at the patio table. Laura and Mr. Wu watched the road. Mr. Wu's eyes followed the tree line, sweeping first one way, then the other. Then he was looking right at them. He had seen them in the shadows. He began walking toward them—something he would not have done if he were trying to warn them off.

He entered the trees and nodded to Frank. He put out his hand to Doña Mariana. She took it and placed it on her thigh, over the wet dress. She drew her boots out of the stirrups. He put his left shoe—a black slipper—in the stirrup, grabbed the saddle horn and—as she leaned forward—swung up behind her. Then she took his hands and placed one on each thigh. He dropped his face so that his mouth and nose were against her neck. She turned her head so that her nose was against his ear.

Frank did not look away. He did not look to one side. He had never seen people care for each other so much.

He felt some jealousy, but it was more like envy of what there could be between two people. That is when something happened to him, a kind of clarity, an understanding within himself, that these were special people and that he cared for them because they cared for each other.

He glanced down at his Winchester. He studied the two screws that held the steel cap against the end of the rifle butt. He would use this thing, not just to protect himself in a dangerous world. Now he saw it as something to use to protect others. That was the difference. Such caring required something of him.

He had lost one friend, but still had these two. And although he was so much younger, a feeling came over him as might come over a young father who knows he will do whatever he has to do to protect his wife and children and all those he loves.

Still keeping Mr. Wu's hands under hers, pressed against the tops of her thighs, Doña Mariana turned in the saddle, to look at Frank.

"Frank," she said. "This is my dear friend Wu Lian," and then she stopped, even though it seemed she had intended to say more.

Frank knew perfectly well who he was, without the other name, of course. He thought about her kiss when he was lying on his bed next to Sofía de Larousse. She had leaned forward and kissed him on the lips, nightgown open at the top. He tried to remember how much he had seen, if anything at all. She had shown concern. She had been inviting, more in a complete sense, not just what had to do with his nakedness and hers. The same invitation was there now, in her eyes. Join us, we are people who care for you.

He straightened in his saddle, glanced toward the house and the road that led up to it. Laura and Manuelito were hurrying across the field toward them. He turned to Mr. Wu and said, "I am very glad to meet you, sir."

Doña Mariana breathed out, and he thought she looked relieved.

Mr. Wu's attention was already on Laura and Manuelito. The riders moved forward to meet them. When Laura was still twenty feet away, she said there was a young, sick woman lying in front of the icehouse. Someone must have left her there, because it looked like she couldn't walk herself. She was weak and feverish. Through an opening in her largely unbuttoned dress you could see she had a rag bandage high on one thigh.

When they reached the icehouse, Frank recognized her. He explained quickly. The camp above the swimming hole, the Jefe arresting them, the thigh wound, the maggots. "Her name is Antonia," Frank said.

Her eyes were red with fever. She kept them on Frank. Mr. Wu knelt beside her, rubbed his hands together, then swept them over the young woman, beginning at her head and ending over her bare, soiled feet, without touching her. They carried her to the patio and made a bed for her on the table where Frank received his treatments in the shade of the grape arbor.

Mr. Wu opened the bandage. Laura made a face and turned away. Mr. Wu said the wound looked good. He said the little white friends could work some more. He rebandaged her, then made a tea from some of his herbs and held her head up while she sipped it. He said the tea would bring down her fever. She needed rest and security, he said.

At the breakfast table, under the ancient oak, Laura fed everyone eggs and tortillas. Manuelito sat on a box on top of a chair and drank goat's milk, this time with chocolate in it. Sofía de Larousse came downstairs in a simple gray dress. She looked rested. She had pulled her hair back in a knot and wore no accents on her lips or eyes. It was as if Frank did not exist. Her eyes never quite found him.

Frank went to the stables. He worked quickly. He got hay and water for Tosca. She ate and drank while he worked. He made a canvas roll of hay to bend over his saddlebags. He checked the magazine in his Winchester. He went up to his room and got the two boxes of shells from the top drawer of his dresser. He packed the telescope. He laid out a clean shirt and a pair of pants. It was really all he had. He wrapped everything in the clean shirt. He said goodbye to the room and all that had happened in it, pulled the door shut behind him and went down the back stairs. He passed Laura, who looked concerned, maybe even worried for him.

Back in the stables, he packed everything in his saddlebags and led Tosca outside. He took out the telescope and stood behind her head, so the others would not see what he was doing. Mr. Wu appeared beside him. He carried an elongated bundle wrapped in black silk. Frank saw the notched tip of a bow sticking out the end.

He swept the telescope slowly along the horizon. Neither spoke. Frank thought his friend could probably see what he was seeing, but without the glass. A wisp of dust rose over the road at some distance. They were probably riders, but the trees in-between still hid them.

"I think they're coming," said Mr. Wu.

He turned to Frank, who had lowered the telescope. Mr. Wu held up his hands and slowly pressed his palms against Frank's cheeks.

"You will be better," he said. "Be careful of the judgments you make at first. Do the movements I taught you, each morning." And then he went off, with the silk-wrapped bow under his arm.

Mariana's three vaqueros came quickly, choosing the field over the road, so as not to raise dust. So no one would think they had been on guard. They galloped around the back of the house. Doña Mariana gave them instructions. Frank sat on Tosca . . . waiting. The men lifted young Antonia up onto the horse and arranged her so that she sat sidesaddle in front of Frank, who reached around to hold her steady. Laura handed over the *rebozo* from her own shoulders. Samuel tied Frank and Antonia together around the waist, so she would be less likely to lose her seat, and so Frank could use both arms if he had to.

"This is Antonia," Frank said to the vaqueros.

"We know," said Samuel.

Frank didn't ask how they knew. Mr. Wu gave him his hand. "We can explain Juan Carlos—since he's dead—but not you, and certainly not Antonia."

"Go now," Doña Mariana said, laying a hand on his knee. "And do not forget us."

Frank looked at everyone, quickly. He wanted to say he loved them all, but instead he said, "Manuelito, don't forget to drink your goat's milk." His eyes sought, then found, those of Doña Mariana and, finally, Sofía de Larousse. He turned Tosca and, as slowly as he could, cantered with Antonia to the woods. He stopped in the shadows long enough to see who was approaching the house—then went deeper into the forest.

CHAPTER 22

Green Bottle Flies

Doña Mariana went in the back door. The vaqueros walked around to the front of the house. Sofía de Larousse climbed the back stairs, went to her room and held up the dress she had worn at the station. Doña Mariana watched from the front door. The two Rurales came first, and behind them six Carrancista soldiers dressed in khaki, mounted and armed. Last, because of the smell, presumably, came a mule and wagon—different this time—and the tin coffin with Sofía de Larousse's husband. The wagon driver held a handkerchief to his mouth and nose.

They stopped in front of the house. Doña Mariana and her three vaqueros walked forward to greet the visitors. The vaqueros carried their rifles in the crooks of their arms. The six troopers fanned out in a semicircle. The sun was warm, the air began to move, and soon the smell of Sofía de Larousse's husband reached them all. A thin cloud of green bottle blowflies hummed around the bullet holes in the casket.

Doña Mariana greeted the Rurales. They smirked, as if they were too powerful to have to return a courtesy. Sofía de Larousse came out the front door. She had quickly put on her black mourning dress. She stepped forward and stood beside Doña Mariana. For a moment, no one spoke. The Rurales scanned the house. Doña Mariana followed their eyes. Mr. Wu stood at the front door.

"That's my servant Mr. Wu," she said. "I think you know him."

She looked back at the Rurales. The one in charge was Jesús Muñoz Galván. She had known him most of her life. He had always been a bully, and there had been an incident the year before when he had been found trying to undress a boy of six from one of the poorer parts of the city.

Mr. Wu had already decided the soldiers looked only semi-regular. Their uniforms did not match, from one to the other, or even between tops and bottoms on the same man. It was likely, he thought, that Jesús and his *compadre* had selected men they already had some connection with, who now slumped in their saddles like people who had come to plunder and saw no need to put on airs.

"Jesús," Doña Mariana inquired, "is there any chance they could unload the coffin in front of the icehouse. I now think we should bury Captain Saúrez here and not in Mexico City, for the obvious reasons."

Jesús nodded to the wagon driver, who gave the mule a flap of the reins and moved off toward the right of the house, taking the cloud of blowflies with him. Immediately, the air improved.

"It was kind of you to bring him. Very kind," said Sofía de Larousse. And then she bowed her head and let out a sigh. Doña Mariana put an arm around her waist.

The six troopers looked back and forth between the two women, the Chinaman in his doorway and the armed vaqueros. The troopers' old Springfields were still in their scabbards, *probably a good sign,* thought Mr. Wu, but not conclusive. For all their slouching, they still had not relaxed their knees, the pressure on their horses. If they made their move, they would draw their pistols and drive their horses straight at the vaqueros.

"We've come to see about the gringo," said Jesús.

Doña Mariana had already decided to tell as much of the truth as she thought advisable.

"There was a gringo here," she said, "but he left. I assume he's on his way back north."

The Rurales exchanged looks.

"He was part of the attack," said Jesús. "And he was seen at the river early this morning."

Doña Mariana calculated quickly. She decided neither Father Ibarra nor the ox driver would have said anything. It had to be someone watching from a distance. And at a distance, they could have been mistaken.

"It could have been Mr. Wu at the river. He has light skin. As far as the attack goes, we heard the Villistas took along a young gringo and a Mexican doctor. They were prisoners, probably held so they could warn no one. The doctor was killed. The gringo escaped."

The Rurales considered her reply. "We will search the house," said Jesús.

"I'd prefer you didn't, Jesús," said Doña Mariana. "I'd prefer you didn't poke around in my bedroom or treat my young servant with the disrespect you showed her in town. You can take my word for it, he is not here. Further, I believe the new constitution forbids a search without just cause and a judge's order. If you do have the written order, I would be glad, of course, to look at it."

Watching from his house, Mr. Wu noticed that the three vaqueros had gradually moved away from each other. There were now up to three yards between each of them, a spread that could have the turning effect of a fence if the soldiers charged. The vaqueros' line of fire would be more open. They could be sure of bringing down several middle horses with the first volley. The resulting chaos would turn both flanks outward and away from them.

"You know," said Doña Mariana, "there's no need for bad feelings. You are all brave men. We all love México. Plus, the authorities in Mexico City—by which I mean Carranza himself—frown on taking the law into one's own hands. There can be severe consequences, as we have seen."

CHAPTER 23

Pig Hitch

Frank, on Tosca with Antonia in front of him, followed the path through the first thick grove of *pirules* and cottonwoods. He had not gone thirty feet when Gray Braids stepped out onto the path from one side and Merce from the other, each holding an old Mauser at hip level.

"There are Rurales and a group of Carrancistas approaching the house," he said. "Juan Carlos the doctor is dead."

Berta's face fell. She glanced up the trail toward the house. Then the women moved quickly. They gathered up their bedrolls and sacks. They had planned to stay close to Antonia for a while, said Berta. She led them farther into the woods. They found a bush-covered hollow they could defend. They tucked Antonia into it and covered her with blankets. Frank said he was going to have a look. He would be back in a half hour.

"We don't have watches," said Berta.

"I'll be back shortly," said Frank.

He rode Tosca through the trees until he figured he had a line of sight that would include what was happening in front of the house. Then he dismounted and crawled forward to where he could use the telescope. His head was heavy from lack of sleep and still hurt from the rifle blow.

The sun was high. He lay deep in the shade of pepper trees and scrub oak, twenty feet back from the tree line. There was little chance that the sun could reflect off the old brass telescope. Heat waves distorted what he was looking at. He watched the two Rurales dismount, and their legs appeared rubbery, changing, sometimes separated at the knees. The six Carrancistas—soldiers-of-fortune, Frank decided—were mounted on an assortment of neglected beasts. Then he saw the Rurales draw their revolvers, the troops point their rifles. The head Rural yelled something at the vaqueros, who hesitated. They looked over at Doña Mariana, who was saying something back. Slowly, the vaqueros placed their rifles on the ground.

Frank couldn't see Mr. Wu but knew he would be watching everything that was going on. There was the bow, a short thing with reverse curves. Mr. Wu had made it. He had said Ghengis Khan had built an empire using a combination of small fast horses and this kind of bow. Frank had seen Mr. Wu practice, nocking the arrow without looking at it, lifting the bow from a contained stance, elbows close to the body, never leaving the forward armpit exposed and, as Mr. Wu had described it—with calm breathing, thinking no hurry—only releasing the arrow when the arrow said so.

Frank had seen him puncture a tin can lid at forty paces. He had seen him do it standing, running and from one of Doña Mariana's quick mares, riding straight at the target, left shoulder forward, left foot forward, raising the bow, and—as the expression went—splitting the mane, as the arrow sped forward over the horse's head. He had also seen him miss.

He knew Mr. Wu had a supply of arrows. He knew Mr. Wu would not permit harm to anyone in his family—Doña Mariana, Laura and now little Manuelito. Any minute, through the wavering light, Frank expected to see an arrow appear in the chest of one of the Rurales. Then there would be chaos, as Mr. Wu released one arrow after another, aiming first at the horses, then at the men. The vaqueros would pick up their rifles. And the commanding Rural—if he was still standing—would put a bullet in Doña Mariana as one of his first shots.

Frank wriggled backward, got up, stowed the spyglass and mounted Tosca. He didn't really have a plan. He emerged from the tree line at an angle, so that he would come up behind the house and swing around to the left of it. Mr. Wu saw him first, passing by his parlor window. The wagon driver saw him next and took cover behind the wagon and the stinking coffin. Then the Rural, Jesús, saw Frank coming around the corner of the house, holding his arms out and down, showing he would not go for his Winchester.

Doña Mariana slowly shook her head when she saw him. Jesús aimed his pistol. Frank rode straight up to him and turned Tosca so he stood between Jesús and Doña Mariana. He placed his hands on his saddle horn and slouched a little, as if pausing for conversation. He saw Mr. Wu come out the front door.

Mr. Wu carried a quiver of maybe eight or ten arrows, slung at waist level, across his hip. In his right hand he held a short, almost child-sized bow. The same hand also held an arrow.

All of the visitors knew about the Apaches and Comanches their grandfathers had fought. But this was a Chinaman, so no one knew what to make of it, and no one fired at him . . . or even raised a gun. No one even ordered him to keep his distance.

The Chinaman came right up and stood beside Frank's horse. He unstrapped his quiver and laid it on the ground, along with the bow and single arrow. He lay the single arrow down first, and the bow over and perpendicular to it, nocking the arrow as he did so. If he picked it up with his left hand, taking both the bow and the arrow at the same time, he would only have to pull and release.

The appearance of the gringo had changed things. There was no need to search the house. Jesús remounted his horse, and his deputy followed suit. Jesús moved his horse up beside Tosca. He reached down to slide the Winchester out of its scabbard. Frank's right hand, already roughly in that area, came down on top of Jesús' hand and held both the hand and the butt of the Winchester firmly in place.

"This rifle belongs to me," said Frank, politely, as if it were a matter of a mix-up.

He meant to say something about his neutrality and that of the house. That he was only doing what his doctor had told him, get away from the mine. That he had not wanted to be a prisoner of Villa and a target of the Apaches or get hit in the head by the scout's rifle. That all of them had a responsibility to protect everyone present at that very moment.

Jesús grunted an order at his deputy. Nacho, a handsome man with white teeth, rode closer and aimed his Smith & Wesson at arm's length, close to Frank's head. Jesús undid the leather tie holding his rope. He lay the leather tie across his saddle between his crotch and the saddle horn. One end of the rope had a spliced eye, through which he then fed the other end—making a lasso. He dropped the loop over Frank's head, where it hung up on the old canvas hat for a moment before it fell down around his neck.

Instead of giving his speech, Frank reached up slowly. His hands had begun to tremble. He took the lasso back off his head, knocking his hat askew as he did so. He put his hat back in place. Sweat seeped into the corners of his eyes, stinging. He wiped his eyes with the heel of one hand, then the other, switching Jesús' lasso back and forth between his hands while he wiped. Then he dropped the loop over Jesús' own saddle horn and drew it tight, so that Jesús now held his own saddle lassoed.

Nacho thumbed the hammer back on his revolver.

Doña Mariana said, "Nacho, uncock your gun. This man is our friend. He enjoys the protection of this house."

"Well," said Jesús, "he was part of the attack."

"He was a prisoner of the Villistas," said Doña Mariana.

"We can hang him, or we can hang you all," Jesús countered. A vein stood out on his temple as he said it. His eyes had gone bloodshot, maybe from the prisoner unroping himself. His hands also trembled ever so slightly, as he lifted the lasso from his own saddle horn.

"Well, why don't you hang us all," said Doña Mariana, and now veins stood out on her neck too. "As well as Laura and the child inside the house." She stepped closer. "Listen, Jesús, we've known each other all our lives. Think about what you're doing. This man is my guest, and we are not revolutionaries. He is not one of México's enemies."

Jesús spread the loop again and laid it on his lap. "Shoot him if he resists," he said to Nacho. "I mean it. If he moves at all, shoot him. Put your hands back down, gringo."

That's where Frank's hands already were. Jesús bound his wrists with the leather tie. He lifted the wrists and slipped the lasso around them. He cinched the now double-bound wrists to Frank's saddle horn. Frank's hands began to turn white.

"I was a prisoner," said Frank.

"You're a prisoner now, *cabrón*," said Jesús.

"Jesús! Listen to me!" said Doña Mariana.

Jesús made two loops from the standing end of his lasso, lay the loops over each other—reversed—then dropped the loops back over Frank's head, in a clove hitch, and pulled tight, so that Frank was trussed head to wrists, wrists to saddle.

"We call this the pig hitch," said Jesús.

Doña Mariana was protesting. Frank could see her mouth moving. Frank's stomach worked as he tried to breathe. Jesús came in close. He tapped his forefinger on Frank's bound wrists.

"I'll cut these off you, when your hands are black. First we find a telegraph pole. There's a good tree just down the road. We loosen the girth on your horse. You go up along with your saddle. The saddle pulls down on you. You hang."

He played out two yards of the lasso and tied it off on his own saddle horn, so he could lead Frank and his horse. The wind had shifted. Frank could smell Sofía's husband. His head swam. He saw Manuelito at the threshold of the front door. Laura stood behind him. Her smooth Tepehuana arms were crossed over the boy's chest. What had he been thinking to ride back to them this way? His Chinese friend was bending over, sinking out of sight and abandoning him. He felt the warmth of the afternoon sun on his crotch, and realized he had wet himself.

He didn't want anyone to see it. He slanted his eyes down toward Doña Mariana. She was not looking at his wet trousers. Mr. Wu rose up again. He must have seen. His hand came up and rested on Frank's thigh. The hand squeezed him three times.

"Please leave these people alone," Frank rasped.

Jesús' eyes widened with interest.

"This is their home. They are peaceful people." This last remark came out almost as a sob. His eyes had begun cloud.

"Cry for your mother," said Jesús, looking at Doña Mariana.

Sofía stood beside Frank and squeezed his Achilles tendon through his boot.

Two figures in long stained tan skirts came walking around the left side of the house. They carried their old Mausers slung over their shoulders, showing they didn't intend to use them. Frank thought he recognized Berta and Merce.

"What the fuck is this?" said Jesús.

The women had crossed half the distance from the house when the wagon driver came running around the right side of the house, and there was something coming behind him. Maybe the wagon, the coffin and the mule—all moving back toward them. The sound increased, now more like rocks in an avalanche. An instant later, some thirty horsemen thundered around the corner, leaning into the curve, rifles in their hands—right on the heels of the wagon driver.

Jesús' troopers didn't know where to point their rifles. They lowered them. Nacho uncocked his shiny Smith & Wesson. The Jefe and a few of his men rode up to Frank. Frank couldn't turn his head to see, but he recognized the voice. He drew a blank on the name. He only remembered him climbing out of the swimming hole, his backside, the swinging testicles.

"Well, Jesús, at it again?" said the Jefe. "Fucking little boys and hanging women? And this time, you've got yourself a gringo. Alas, he's my gringo, and you are in a shitload of trouble."

CHAPTER 24

Recruitment

J esús had grown pale. There were too many rifles pointed at them. The square-jawed Indian woman now pressed the muzzle of her old Mauser up under his rib cage. The Jefe rode around in front of Frank, so Frank could see him. Merce passed up an old bone-handled jackknife. The Jefe tut-tutted as he lifted the pig hitch from Frank's neck. He released Frank's wrists from the saddle horn. Last of all, he cut away the leather tie. He tossed the knife back down to Merce. He rubbed Frank's wrists a few times to bring back the circulation. He whistled an unidentifiable tune through his front teeth as he worked. Now and then it sounded something like "Alexander's Ragtime Band".

"Well, gringo, here we are again," he said with a big sigh, as if in disappointment. And then, darkly, with raised mad eyebrows, he said, "Where is my young woman with the maggots you put inside her?"

Both Merce and Berta began to speak at once. They told the Leader where Antonia was, that she was okay, and that the gringo had brought her to them, and that the doctor was dead.

The Jefe nodded, took in the information, then shifted his attention . . . so he did not really hear it when Frank blurted, in a voice that had gone dry, "Thank you, Goat Balls."

The two Apache enforcers from the swimming hole brought their horses up to Frank. The one with lighter skin, who had struck him with the rifle barrel during the attack, leaned over from his saddle, glaring, and drew two fingers across his own neck, just under the jaw, then rode away. The other one's eyes lingered a little longer on Frank, then he too moved away.

Frank's eyes began to focus. Mr. Wu was now six feet away, with left shoulder and left foot forward, the funny bow half-drawn. The owl-feathered arrow pointed down at a forty-five degree angle. The bow had probably been completely drawn at some point. Aimed at Jesús. Mr. Wu's eyes still followed the Apache scouts as they moved away.

Doña Mariana stood just behind, with her hand on Mr. Wu's shoulder, as if she had been telling him to stop. Frank's eyes rested on his Chinese friend's hands. They were perfectly steady. He found himself barely able to think, except that there were things that happen that you don't even see. He wondered how long Mr. Wu had been standing there.

Jesús sat red-faced, glowering—first at Doña Mariana, then at Frank. It still appeared as if he could not see Mr. Wu. The two Apache enforcers, still mounted, went around collecting guns and ammunition from Jesús' contingent—handing them down to Berta and Merce. They bound each man's wrists—in front—with hemp. The Jefe ordered the captives, including Jesús and Nacho—also bound—to form a line facing him. When they were in position, all still mounted, he addressed them.

"I am low on men," he said. "I usually shoot people like you. You know that. Just as you shoot us. But I am going to give each of you a choice. You fight for us, or we put a bullet in your head right now."

He paused to let them think, realizing that a product of fear is paralysis. The sun was hotter, if anything. Frank and Tosca had also not moved. Frank turned Tosca so he could see the new prisoners. Horses stamped their hooves, blew out their noses and swished their tails at flies. Frank counted five pounding heartbeats in his temple, when the Apache—Frank thought of him now as Throat Cutter—rode up to him again and tried to take the Winchester. Without even looking, Frank placed his right hand on the rifle butt and gripped the Indian's fingers with force, until the hand pulled away again.

Someone tugged at his boot. He saw Sofía looking up at him. She shook his boot again, as if to wake him up. He looked down at her.

"Are you alright?" she asked.

"I feel sick," he said.

The tall, handsome man with the full mustache—the one at the swimming hole who had wanted to kill everybody right then and there—flanked the Jefe, and they started toward the prisoners, as if in review. They came to the first of the eight men. Merce handed the Jefe the bone-handled jackknife again.

"I don't have all day," said the Jefe. "Yes, you ride with me. No, this man puts a bullet in your head."

The first man answered quickly. "Yes, my General, I will ride with you."

The second and third also answered yes. The fourth man was Nacho. He answered yes, but with the slightest hesitation.

"At the first sign of disloyalty, I will shoot you. Do you understand?"

Nacho nodded quickly.

When they stopped in front of the fifth man, he said nothing. "Can he talk?" the Jefe asked Nacho. Nacho said he didn't know, but he thought so. The tall man with the Jefe raised a long-barreled revolver.

"Once more, yes or no?" he asked.

"Maybe he can't hear," Frank yelled across at them. He had had enough of this. "Did you ever think of that?" he shouted, fairly spitting out the words.

They all looked over at him. Then, in a flash, the Jefe's escort turned and fired. The man who would not or could not speak fell to his right and backward. His fall ended with his head just touching the ground, boots still caught in the stirrups. His bound wrists rested on his forehead.

The next two men—six and seven—said "*¡Sí!*" quickly. The last man was Jesús, still red-faced and glowering. The Jefe held out the old bone-handled jackknife.

Jesús held out his wrists. The Jefe sawed through the hemp. He refolded the knife and put it in his pocket. He drew out one of his two Smith & Wessons. He held it up at Jesús' forehead.

"Yes or no, Jesús?"

"Yes," said Jesús.

Frank's temple throbbed once. It throbbed again. The sun beat down. The breeze still carried the smell of Sofía's rotting husband. She still held Frank's boot, just above the round of his heel. She felt him jump when the revolver fired.

Jesús' horse lurched sideways, then settled. There was a spot on Jesús' forehead, as if someone had hit him there with a ripe blackberry. His body, at first too surprised to move, found its tipping point and dropped—also to the right. His left boot, still caught in the stirrup, jerked him back and left him only halfway down, except for his head and neck, which had taken an unpleasant angle against the ground. He looked up past them all, up into the deep sky, his sneer gone, the blackberry oozing dark juice.

The Jefe concluded the ceremony by riding the thirty paces back over to Frank. His Smith & Wesson, still out, came in and out of reflection, like a fish rolling in a stream, aimed at Frank's chest.

Frank saw Mr. Wu raise his bow, in a step as formal as a dance.

The Jefe then held his Smith & Wesson up in the air, pointing it skyward. He waved the barrel back and forth, flattened toward his audience, as if he were showing a piece of evidence—or the source of all authority.

"No one is to touch this dumb gringo *hijo de puta,*" he warned.

Whereupon, he holstered his gun and turned to face what no one else seemed to have seen—Mr. Wu with the half-drawn Ghengis Khan bow and the nocked arrow. He held up a forefinger and wagged it, in a gesture that said something between "not necessary" and "bad boy".

Mr. Wu lowered the bow and gave a slight bow.

The Jefe turned to Berta and Merce, and ordered them to cut the new recruits loose. Men threw the bodies of Jesús and the other trooper over the saddles of their own horses, lashed them wrist to knee and to their saddles, so they would not slip when they were under way. Like stuck pigs, both men dripped thick blood from the nose and mouth.

The Jefe addressed Frank again. "The doctor is dead?"

"Thanks to you," said Frank.

The Jefe shook his head and rolled his eyes.

"And please don't tell me you should shoot me once and for all," Frank said.

The Jefe put his right hand on the grip of his right-side Smith & Wesson. It was more like a nervous gesture. He held up his other hand, with a reassuring palm toward Mr. Wu, who had already begun to draw his bow. "I'm not going to shoot your dumb gringo friend."

"Berta and Merce know how to tend the wound," said Frank. "Antonia knows the herbs Mr. Wu used for the tea to treat the fever. That's Mr. Wu with the bow. He is a fine man. She needs good water and as much rest as possible. That's what Juan Carlos—the doctor you killed—said."

The Jefe looked at Berta. She nodded her head in confirmation. "Maggots and rest?" he said to Frank.

"And safety," said Frank.

The Jefe came up closer. Frank thought Goat Balls' eyes had too much pressure behind them.

The two Apache enforcers were arranging the new recruits in the middle of the column, then positioned themselves behind them. *God help the recruit who tried to break his new allegiance,* Frank thought.

The Jefe came closer still. The ribs of his horse pressed against Frank's boot and stirrup.

"You saw her private parts." His pupils were enlarged, as if it were night.

Frank had seen dried blood, old dirt, trail dust, and the shit no one had had time to wash away. The Jefe's face had turned to wood. His horse shifted the weight over its hind legs, moving the rider first one way, then the other. The horse pawed the ground with a front hoof. "I saw sweetness," said Frank. "And I saw a young woman in pain."

The Jefe opened his mouth. Frank saw his yellow teeth below his mustache. A thread of saliva stretched like rubber from one front tooth to the one below it. The eyes crinkled. The pupils had narrowed again. The corners of his mouth—cracked like dry earth—turned up in a smile. He reached out his hand.

Frank looked down at it, hesitating.

The Jefe nodded, as if encouraging a wary dog to come closer. Frank took the hand. The Jefe shook just once, as if sealing a deal. At the same time, he said, "Go home, gringo." Then he turned, tipped his hat to Doña Mariana, added one more spur wound to his horse's flank and took the lead at the head of the column. With Berta and Merce running ahead, the troop disappeared around the right side of the house, toward the woods where Antonia lay hidden.

THAT AFTERNOON, the three vaqueros dug a hole just at the tree line. With rags over their mouths and noses, they dumped and poured the contents of the tin coffin into the grave. Then they filled it in. Last, they shoveled up the blood from Jesús and the man who could not talk that had soaked the earth in front of the house.

The wagon driver washed out the coffin. Sofía said he could keep it. He thanked her and said he thought he could repair the bullet holes in it. Doña Mariana had known the man for many years; she felt sure he would keep to himself what he had seen. He assured her he would.

She and Mr. Wu agreed that someone would come looking for Jesús and Nacho and the others. The wagon driver said he would tell people that Jesús and his men had been ambushed, then kidnapped, by a random group of Villistas. If anyone asked, he would say he himself had been allowed to go on because of the awful smell coming from the casket.

He said people would believe him because forced conscription was common and because almost everyone disliked and feared Jesús and Nacho. Everyone knew about Jesús and the young boy. Plus, people suspected Jesús and his troopers of irregular dealings. They extorted soldiers' wives. They would produce decayed or otherwise disfigured bodies, with tags that said they were this or that woman's husband or son. She would have to pay a fee. Otherwise the Carrancista government would be obliged to dispose of the body in a mass grave. If the widow or mother paid the fee, she got the body for the wake and burial.

Doña Mariana thanked him again, but the man had not quite finished. There were worse things. There was another soldier, he said, who had already been buried and grieved for—the corpse delivered to the widow by Jesús and Nacho. But the same soldier—not dead at all—was on his way home for a leave. Jesús and his band got wind of it, lay in wait for him and shot him dead. Then they burned and disfigured his body and sold him to another family of means, claiming it was their son.

Doña Mariana asked whether there were witnesses, in case she had to use this information in the future. The driver replied there were, and that Father Ibarra knew who they were.

CHAPTER 25

Snake Mouth

For the rest of the afternoon—after Frank had washed and changed—they sat under the grape arbor in the mottled light, feeling the afternoon breeze coming down from the hills smelling of grass and mesquite, once again clean and reassuring. Later, as the night chilled, they moved inside and sat in front of the hooded Spanish fireplace in the *sala*. The framed daguerreotype of Doña Mariana and her dead son and husband stood on the piano. There was just enough light hitting the photograph and Frank was sitting just close enough, on the couch, to see the man's gold watch chain and the top of his gun belt.

Manuelito curled up on his left, leaning against Frank like a cat seeking warmth and connection. He held Frank's left hand and moved it around as it were a doll to be molded into shape. Tears hung in Frank's eyes. They neither flowed nor went away no matter how much he dabbed at them with the heel of his palm. Mr. Wu came up behind him and rubbed his neck and shoulders. Manuelito got up, went away, and came back with a stuffed cloth dog that he placed on Frank's lap, so it too could be close. Or so Frank could be close to it.

Laura sat on the other side of Manuelito, her knees together and her hand holding the child's bare ankle. Frank glanced into her eyes and saw a person he could not categorize. Different from him by nature of her Indianness but at the same time warm and accessible because of the steadiness with which she looked at him.

Sofía came downstairs, her pupils tiny and dark from more of the purple smoke, her hair pulled tight in a bun at the back of her head. She wore a grey dress with black stockings visible at her ankles. She sat down on the other side of Frank and spread the folds of her dress so that they touched his hip. When she crossed her legs, more of the black stockings showed. She laid her right hand on the top of her elevated knee. Her left hand fell between her leg and Frank's, resting on the material of her dress, palm up. Frank's gaze fell on the area on her leg where her ankle began to curve up into her calf. He glanced at her face. Her lids were heavy. She stared at the fire—as if lost in thought.

Doña Mariana brought in a crystal carafe of brandy. Only she and Frank drank. She kept her eyes on him. The man had offered himself in order to save the rest of them. Jesús had been ready to hang him. She wondered whether he realized that she and Mr. Wu and the vaqueros would not have let that happen.

When Frank lowered his glass after the first sip, he saw her looking at him—her gaze unwavering—and tears filled his eyes again.

Later, while Laura washed his trousers, Doña Mariana and Mr. Wu drew Frank a bath, made him undress and ran washcloths, heavy with warm water, over his back. They washed his hair and spoke quietly with one another while Frank hung his head forward and surrendered to their touch.

That night, which would be his last at the house, he lay on his back, naked under the down quilt Doña Mariana had given him against the cold. He was exhausted and, relaxed by the brandy, welcomed the sleep that was overtaking him, when the door opened and Sofía entered his room. She lit the candle beside the bed, and without looking at him, took off her robe and slipped her white body in next to his and laid a thigh over his stomach. She inched up along him and kissed him on the lips. Then she got on top of him and moved back and forth on him until, with a motion of her hand, she had him inside her.

Frank had never really found himself in that place, including with Rosa Marta who had said that that would require a more formal arrangement.

The warmth and moisture concerned him. The brandy delayed any decision as to what to do. She told him to remain still and not think about anything, least of all about that afternoon. Just feel good, let me make love to you. Forget everything that has happened.

Frank relaxed. He admired the candlelight on her white breasts, the curve of her belly against his. She reached up and pulled the bun out of her hair, and the sides of her face were now hidden in shadow. She made slow, lower register sounds. Now and then she trembled—inside and out.

When they had finished, he at least—with some low register sounds of his own—Frank felt a confidence and an intimacy he had never known and—viewing honesty as a good thing—told her that it was probably he, Frank, who, with his Winchester, at a very long range, one week ago to the day, had shot her husband.

Sofía stopped moving. She was propped over him and now let herself down so that her head rested sideways on his chest. He reached up to move some of her hair so he could see her eyes, but the angle of her hair and forehead still blocked his view. She lay perfectly still, and if Frank had had more experience, he might have known that she wasn't asleep.

The candle wavered in the occasional movement of soft, chilled night air coming through the window. He closed his eyes and felt his breathing lifting and lowering her gently, as if she were a boat and he the water.

When he opened his eyes again, it took him a moment to understand what had changed. She had her robe on again and sat over his groin, as she had before. Except that this time she held—with both hands—a small shiny object that reflected the light of the candle and was aimed roughly at his nose.

He wondered if it had a pearl handle. He could see the single opening—a black snake mouth.

She had returned her hair to its former bun, looser, higher up this time and held in place by an ivory hair comb that came to a peak over the crown of her head. Her pupils had changed and were larger, so Frank concluded she had not smoked more of her brown paste.

He studied her, as she apparently studied him. He did not know how to reconcile the intimacy they had just had with the nickel-plated derringer in her hands. She turned the weapon slightly toward herself, as if puzzling over what she held, or that she still held it.

Frank had never exchanged many words with Sofía, nor really with women in general, and so he did not know how to proceed. His lips were dry and the muscles of his mouth were frozen, yet he managed to say—in a rasping voice, "Have I offended you somehow?"

The door to the bedroom opened. Light from a new source warmed the doorframe, followed by a wrist, a candle and then Doña Mariana. Her dark hair, held away from her forehead by a band of silver, fell over her shoulders and down over the robe, curving inward at the top of her bosom. She stood still, holding her free hand in back of the candle so it did not blind her.

Sofía did not move, but still aimed the derringer at Frank's face, waving it slowly from one corner to another in a square drawn from Frank's eyes to the corners of his mouth. She would have to shoot him between the eyes and about two inches higher for the small caliber bullet to kill him, he thought.

He glanced past his executioner-to-be. The second one in less than twelve hours. Doña Mariana stood still. Did she understand why they weren't moving? Did his eyes tell her what was happening? He knew she could not see the derringer.

"Sofía," said Doña Mariana, "is everything alright?"

Sofía raised her shoulders and dropped them. Then she was still again.

"Sofía," Doña Mariana asked, "what should I do to help you?"

Sofía shrugged her shoulders again. "He killed my husband," she said.

Doña Mariana had come closer and now could see the derringer.

Frank watched Sofía's eyes for a sign of softening. But, with one hand, she thumbed back the hammer and pressed the little gun against the correct spot on his forehead.

"Your husband was about to kill a boy in the mountains," said Doña Mariana. "Frank was watching from a ridge. He saw a mounted officer about to shoot a boy of nine or ten, who was herding goats in the mountains. Your husband was going to shoot a boy who limped. The boy was throwing stones at your husband because your husband was trying to steal his goats."

Sofía's shoulders sank a little. She moved the derringer an inch higher and pressed the muzzle against his skin—with slightly less pressure.

"Frank is your friend," Doña Mariana continued. "You held his boot when they wanted to hang him. He has never taken advantage of you. He got you away from the train station. He was tender toward your husband while he was dying. He took a quick, long distance shot from the ridge, in a situation where you would have done the same thing."

Sofía let out something between a growl and a sob. The derringer had moved to Frank's hair line. Still a spot for final damage.

"I could marry you," said Frank, who thought that was what having sex might imply. Doña Mariana shook her head. It was not something she would have said in that moment.

"You don't even know me," said Sofía.

"You're a beautiful woman," said Frank.

"I'm an opium addict. I live in Mexico City, I don't speak English . . . and you're a cowboy."

"I'm a mining engineer," said Frank. "You could learn English."

"You have mercury poisoning," said Sofía.

"He was going to let them hang him, to save us," said Doña Mariana.

"My husband was a bastard," said Sofía, and uncocked the derringer. She held it out to one side. Doña Mariana took it gently. She went to the open window and tossed it out into the darkness. All three of them heard it hit the ground. If it had remained cocked, it would have gone off, Frank thought.

Sofía lay her head back down on Frank's chest. "I'm sorry," she said, to the universe, and began to cry.

Frank wanted to say the same thing, but instead pulled the down quilt up around them with his arms around her. Doña Mariana came over. She held her robe together at the top so it would not fall open. She kissed Frank on the forehead, about where the bullet would have entered. She blew out their candle.

"We'll have breakfast together tomorrow," she said. Then she opened the door, turned, and backed out. Candlelight warmed the door frame, and then the door closed.

CHAPTER 26

Grebe Spray

At breakfast, outside in back, Sofía sat apart from Frank. She did not look at him. No one talked about the previous afternoon. As they passed *gorditas* back and forth, Manuelito asked if more soldiers would come that day. Doña Mariana said she thought they'd had enough soldiers for a while. Frank knew the vaqueros were watching the road from the front of the house.

Afterward, he brought Tosca around. He hugged everyone—except Laura, who stood by the back door and would not come forward.

She twisted her hands. Doña Mariana's eyes were moist. When he hugged Sofía, she remained stiff, her arms at her sides.

"It doesn't feel like I should be leaving," said Frank, though everyone, including him, knew that they would always be in danger as long as he stayed and the troubles continued.

Mr. Wu handed him a package of green tea and reminded him to do the movements for Coiling Silk for his health, each morning and each evening. His hug was strong and warm. Sofía did not stand next to Tosca. She did not hold his boot. Frank kept looking at her. She did not look back. He even glanced at her hands, wondering where the derringer was. Then he clucked Tosca forward and looked away.

When he reached the edge of the field, he waved. The others waved back—even Sofía. Then he rode through the trees and turned onto the path that led along beside the Chuviscar, going east.

He passed the sandbank where they had burned Juan Carlos, then took the trail off to the left, through the pines and red earth. Letting Tosca drink at the swimming hole, he listened carefully to be sure no one was there, then knelt beside Tosca and drank.

He filled his canteen and rode between the boulders and the cliffs, through the field where they had filled Antonia's wound with maggots, then entered the woods again.

Before he was too far along, he stopped and looked back to see if anyone was following him. He saw no one. In another fifteen minutes he stopped again. Watching. Depending on the weather, a tracker had up to several hours to start after him. He would watch from high points along the way, in places where he could see for a long distance. Over and over, as he rode on, Frank relived what had happened. His heart was heavy, his thinking troubled.

On the second day he thought about Kipling's *Captain Courageous,* his father's favorite book. Everything Frank knew about the high seas came from this book, which his father used to read to him before bed. In rough weather, a helmsman might or might not see another ship across an expanse of gray sky and green water. It depended whether the following, pursuing ship rose to the top of a storm swell, or wallowed dangerous and unseen in the trough between crests.

He stopped on a high pine ridge, dismounted and lay down with his brass telescope propped across a rock, then looked out across the distances. How many times had he done this already? Every fifteen minutes at first. Then gradually, every hour. The morning sun fell across his back and warmed him. There were always people moving through the countryside, some on foot, some on burros, some—once in a while—on horseback. He discounted the importance of anyone on foot or burro. On the other hand, a horse and rider could mean trouble. And trouble would come along the ridges or gullies he had traveled. So he spent time reconstructing his path, picking out, the best he could, the way he had come.

It was not too difficult. In an hour, he did not cover that much ground. There were only so many ridgelines, turns of river, criss-crossing dirt wagon roads or trails. The trick was predicting how a tracker might follow him without showing himself. He would make a sighting, then let Frank go on. He would rely on Tosca's tracks and general knowledge of Frank's direction. Someone familiar with the country, or not, could ride parallel to Frank, at some distance—maybe a mile away—knowing that later on he would see Frank on an open piece of ground, ideally a little behind, and could then set up an ambush.

Frank cut an apple in half, got up, and held it out to Tosca in a cupped hand. She took it happily, nibbling at his palm with rubbery lips, leaving it sweet with apple juice and saliva. He wiped his hand on the back of his pants, took a bite of his half of the apple, and, chewing, lay down for one more look.

A spot of water came into view. A pond of some sort. He had not seen it on his way. A breeze caught the surface so that it reflected the dark blue of the sky. Small water birds—grebes of some sort—fed among the pond's rushes. They splashed, dunked their heads, disappeared completely under water, then re-emerged, rising out of the water as if standing and flapped their wings so that for an instant, a fine spray sparkled around them. Frank moved the glass slowly, relishing the interplay of birds, water and light.

On the bank behind them, stood two horses, saddled, dozing in the sun, tied up to nothing at all—one Appaloosa mare and one sorrel gelding, both of which looked familiar. Frank moved the glass to the right and saw a third horse, a black mare that looked like one of Doña Mariana's. He moved the glass farther to the right, past the horses, and saw the Jefe's two Apaches, sitting with their backs to trees, their eyes closed, apparently resting. And two trees farther, also sunning but looking approximately in his direction, sat Sofía de Larousse, dressed in khaki, with riding boots and a floppy canvas trail hat.

My grandfather wrote that his heart froze when he saw them. If it had been Sofía alone, that would have been one thing, but together with the two Apaches, that made his stomach drop.

Embarrassment rushed to his face. Perhaps the reluctant murderer of Captain Saúrez was not to escape after all. He imagined them willing to skin him alive, or hang him over fire, or just hang him from some young ash tree beside a blue pond where grebes would go on splashing, producing glitter, long after he stopped jerking, his pants dark with urine.

His first impulse was to run. He wasn't even an hour ahead of them. Sofía would not be able to keep up. The scouts would not stay back with her. They would force her horse along with a lead rope.

There was too much he did not understand. Had the scouts broken with Pancho Villa? Would they have dared to do that? Had the Jefe sent them, ordered them to deliver Sofía to the man she wanted to be with? Or had she herself contracted the Apaches and paid them to hunt him down and dispense justice?

He raised the telescope and looked again. The men still slept. He watched them for some time to be sure it wasn't all part of a ruse he did not understand. One of the Apaches now lay on his side, his rib cage rising and falling in sleep. Frank moved the glass to Sofía, beginning high, then going lower. Her eyes were now closed, too. This probably meant she felt comfortable in the company of the men. Her face was clean and not drawn. Her legs were out in front of her. Then he saw it. A cord leading from one ankle across the fifteen feet or so to the scout who was still sitting. The one with the lighter skin.

The knot rode high on her laced riding boot, tight against the black stocking and probably tight enough to take some time to untie. The cord prevented a quick escape. If she somehow slipped the knot, she still wouldn't get away. They would run her down and maybe punish her. She knew that. They knew that. The tether spared them all the trouble.

But what was the point of her being a prisoner? Why didn't she look more haggard? Was she willing bait? If so, then it was a matter of vengeance. The Apaches would get a fine horse, a spyglass and his Winchester. Whatever the plan, the enforcers likely wanted to get it done quickly and get back to the Jefe. But then the Jefe had publicly warned his men to leave the dumb gringo alone. That had to mean they didn't plan to return and felt free to do whatever they wanted. They were running north then, and they meant to snare him on the way. As for Sofía, maybe so much of the brown paste kept her from showing the fear she should have been feeling.

My grandfather wrote that he made a decision at that moment. He would hunt the hunters in self-defense. So he crawled backward, got up, led Tosca back through the pines and mounted.

CHAPTER 27

Mud and Mayhem

When the shadows grew long, he came across a sizeable stream running almost due north. It must have rained upstream. The water was muddy and might make it harder for them to track him. He stayed in the stream, his neck and shoulders tense and sore from continually looking over his shoulder. He wondered whether they had figured out what he was doing and were coming along on the bank where they could move faster. Or, maybe, one of them was riding hard to circle around him and get ahead of him. Except that daylight was failing and moving fast was becoming more difficult. Plus, they didn't know exactly where he was because the country was flat and there were no long views.

There were side creeks, and Frank finally chose one running west that he thought would be right for his purposes. They couldn't check all the side creeks, and he was very careful to keep Tosca in the deepest parts, so that her tracks would be covered by muddy water. When he found a tight grouping of mesquite, he climbed up out of the creek, tied Tosca off and waited.

The light was poor when he saw the Apaches passing in the main stream. He held his breath as he watched, but they had not chosen to come up his side creek. Sofía's horse was in the middle on a lead rope. They did not glance up the long slow grade to where he sat in the mesquite. His pursuers were riding next to each other, their heads close, warning each other not to look up the slope to the grove of mesquite that was probably at the top of the side creek they had just gone by. They passed out of sight. A half hour later, farther north, along the main stream, he saw they had built a small fire and were settling down for the night.

He took out his silver pocket watch. He squinted at the black hands. He laid the watch on the ground rather than putting it back in his pocket, so there would less movement when he reached for it, less rustle from his clothes. So he wouldn't miss a sound he needed to hear.

He thought about waiting and how it was a weapon. He let two hours go by. The two Apache scouts, prized by the Jefe, would be capable of layers of decoy and misdirection. The fire was no simple matter. It gave away their position. It also distorted Frank's night vision if they were walking back toward him on foot. He held up his hand to block out the fire. He looked for signs, perhaps an owl disturbed, flying away a little too quickly, barely discernible against the slightly lighter night sky. He listened for sounds other than those of the creek or Tosca shifting positions. He watched her ears, to see if she was hearing something. He drew air in slowly through his nostrils for the smell of wood smoke, which would be clinging to the Apaches' clothes. He studied the horizon in all directions, especially the area that was downwind from him, because that was the way they would come. For better night vision, he looked just to one side of shapes, trying to determine whether he was looking at, say, a cactus stump or a man standing frozen looking back at him.

He got the dark oilskin poncho out of his saddlebag and put it on with the hood down so he could hear and see, then took off his old canvas hat and tucked it in a saddlebag and went to the creek and smeared mud on his face and hands. He could hear Tosca smelling him, breathing in and out through her nose, as she puzzled out the meaning of the mud.

He untied the Winchester and slipped it out of its scabbard, then filled a canvas pouch with extra shells and hung it over his head and one shoulder. He tried to thumb a shell into the rifle's side loading gate, but the cartridge would not go in. The magazine was already full. Thirteen cartridges end to end, lined up in the steel tube under the barrel, each one waiting to be levered back into the firing chamber. Each one lethal.

He tied the neck of the ammunition bag and told Tosca he would be back in a bit. Putting his head against her for a moment, he stroked her neck, then loosened her lead rope at the mesquite tree. If something happened to him and she got hungry, she could pull loose and find her way to an appreciative owner.

He set off down the slope, through the cactus and scrub, keeping the face of the wind between him and the fire so they would not smell him coming—the mud, the gun oil, the sweat of a gringo.

He squatted now and then, so he could look up against the horizon and see a profile that otherwise wasn't apparent. He listened. He smelled. He walked again. They could be waiting for him. Sofía would be the bait, tied down near the fire. Unless, of course, they were working for her to settle the old score—his life for her husband's. They could put things under their blankets to make him think they were sleeping, but be waiting for him outside the light of the fire. And anyway, why was the fire still burning? Why hadn't they pissed on it and gone to sleep, if they hadn't wanted to draw him in?

The wind's angle forced him into the main creek. The gurgle of water drowned out the slosh of his steps. He kept to shallow water and sand whenever possible, so he would not trip. He stayed in the creek. Wet boots, out of water, would squish and give him away.

He found a high spot and crawled up onto it and lay among *pirul* trees. It was another two hundred feet to the orange of the fire. He wrapped a piece of cloth around the telescope's brass, so it would not reflect. What appeared to be Sofía lay on the ground, under a blanket, to the left of the fire. He kept the glass moving. He studied the two forms lying to the right of the fire. The shapes weren't quite right and never moved. And so he waited. The sound of the water in the creek made him tired, and then it made him afraid because he could not hear if someone was coming up behind him. He regretted that he and Tosca had not just ridden all night, high up against the beginning of the mountains to the west, and kept on running. Except that there was really no way to get away from the men who followed him. They would snare him somewhere. Here, or somewhere close by.

His body ached from not moving. He felt his heart beating against the earth. He thought how small his was and how big Tosca's was. Then he saw them. They emerged from the shadows beyond the fire, now no more than coals. They had been waiting for him, and now appeared to have decided he wasn't coming. Or they were pretending. They walked softly. One laid his rifle down close by, quietly, then lay down and drew a blanket over himself. The other walked over to the lump on the left side of the fire. He laid his rifle down, unbuckled his belt heavy with the hunting knife, slipped off his trousers and got under the blanket.

Frank heard Sofía cry out. It sounded like protest. She appeared to be struggling. Or was it all just one more layer of the deception? To bring him in? Then he heard a clean, fiery snap. And the roar of rage from her assailant, who got to his knees, both hands pressed against his forehead, and howled.

Frank took the spyglass away from his eye. This was no drama they had invented. Sofía had shot the man with her derringer. The other Apache leapt up, his blanket falling away. In her riding dress and boots, Sofía made a run for it, but the line tied to her foot brought her down hard. She got up and faced her captors, snarling like a trapped animal.

The wounded man, naked from the waist down, stood up, swayed and began turning in circles. His partner picked up a rock big enough to smash a head and rushed toward them. Sofía shrieked. Frank fired, and missed entirely. The man with the rock stopped and turned toward him, looking for him in the shadows. Frank levered the Winchester. The man heard him and threw himself on the ground. But the next bullet caught him in his foot, and he screamed.

Frank looked quickly in back of him to see if there were sweepers closing the trap, coming up behind him. He saw nothing moving. Confused, the rock thrower was hopping toward the line of *pirules* they had been hiding in, away from his rifle. The next shot hit him low. He screamed and fell onto his knees. He put a hand where he had been hit and continued crawling toward the trees, exposing his backside. Frank fired at it. The man leapt forward like a frog, dropped onto his stomach and did not move.

The victim of Sofía's little derringer was still turning in circles. Frank looked back, but nothing moved behind him. The circling man circled toward Sofía. He held his hand at a spot between his forehead and his temple and raged as if something hot still burned away at him. Sofía raised her arm as if she had a second shot to fire. Frank ran toward them. The man staggered forward. Sofía screeched, threw the empty derringer at him . . . and hit him. His hand went to his nose, and he stood for a moment, looking at her, at last realizing who was causing him his pain.

From fifty feet away Frank shot and missed him entirely. The man turned toward him, swaying. Still coming, Frank levered and fired from his waist and caught some part of the man's stomach. The man fell backward. Sofía, still tethered, rushed forward and kicked him. The man grabbed her foot. A few more strides, and Frank struck the man's arm with the butt of the Winchester. On the back swing, he struck him in the head.

Then he heard it, the sound of something coming at them from behind. He swung around, saw the horse, and fired—first the horse, then the rider. It screamed and then, standing in one place, began striking the ground with all four feet in a staggered death rhythm. But there was no rider, there were no other horses. The animal he saw slowly drop in front of him was Tosca, who had broken loose and come to be with him.

Frank began to wail. He knelt beside the animal's head and wailed more. He spoke words to her. He rocked back and forth on his knees, his hands over his face. He stroked her forehead. He cursed himself. Her sounds broke his heart. And then he lay down on his stomach, so that the angle was right, and—as was his duty—shot her between her eyes.

He looked back at Sofía. She had picked up the derringer and, with shaking hands, was trying to reload it.

"It's me," he sobbed, getting up. "For God's sake, it's me."

She stopped loading and stared at him, trying to make sense of the mud and the poncho.

"Frank," he said.

Still sobbing, he got up. He levered another round into the firing chamber. He walked over to the dazed half-naked man, who had been derringer-ed twice and was struggling to get to his feet, and shot him in the head. Then he walked over to the rock thrower, who still moved and was saying something. He estimated where the man's heart was and fired two rounds through his back, bouncing him against the earth. Then he walked quickly back to the derringer victim, who lay looking up, his mouth moving. He fired into the man's heart. He chambered a round and fired again. He levered again and heard the firing pin snap against nothing.

He sat down on a rock. "Thirteen," he said, snuffling, and untied the canvas cartridge sack.

He looked around as he fed cartridges into the magazine. Sofía, her foot still tethered, came over and stood beside him. She laid a hand on his shoulder. The hand fluttered. Frank shook uncontrollably.

"There are no others," she said. "There were just three of us."

But Frank continued inserting shells until the magazine took no more. Then he cried for a long time, with her standing beside him, holding his head against her belly. Finally, when the spasms had quieted, without standing or looking up, he reached out and took her hand in his.

CHAPTER 28

Horse Warmth

A sliver of moon rose up through the *pirules* at the edge of the creek, and it got cold. They slept close to each other, fully clothed. Frank lay with his back against Tosca's still-warm belly, with two blankets over them—his and one from the scouts, which smelled of wood smoke. Tosca lay on a slight incline. The blood from the two wounds he had given her flowed away from where they lay. When they were spooned, Sofía reached back and took his hand and placed it over her breast.

They lay that way for some time without speaking. Frank's mind raced. His stomach was tight. He worried about how long it would take for the cold to penetrate up from the ground. His head hurt, as if something had hit him. Did the scout with the rock throw it at him? Had a bullet ricocheted, or was it the horror of what he had done? To the scouts and Tosca.

Sofía jerked at the edge of sleep. She pulled Frank's hand more firmly over her breast.

"I came after you," she said.

Frank considered the information. He was pretty sure he knew what she meant.

"Did you hear what I said?" she asked, turning her head partly back toward him.

Frank nodded, his chin against the top of her head. He was considering what he wanted to say when she jerked again—and was asleep.

Frank did not sleep. He listened to the stream. He listened to the three living horses tethered to *pirules* thumping the earth. He felt Tosca's warmth lessen and the ground chill increase. He considered how they slept. Sofía against him. The two scouts separately and cold. He had killed them. What had he thought would happen if he confronted them? "They cut off faces," was the last thing Berta had said to him in front of the house. "Do not let them near you." He thought of his friend Juan Carlos and Mr. Leibniz. Had he murdered them, or was it a fair fight? How was killing different from murder? And who was responsible?

He awoke when it was just beginning to gray. He extracted himself slowly from between Tosca, who was cold, and Sofía, who was warm. He wrapped the blankets tighter around her. He looked at her face and felt something he had never felt before. You'll know, he heard his father saying. He supposed this was what his father meant.

He turned to Tosca. She had given him her last warmth. Her eyes were open and unmoving, just beginning to cloud. He stood over her and looked at every part of her, so he would remember her. He bowed his head and told her he loved her and that she had been a dear friend. Then he took a big breath and turned away, treading softly so he would not wake Sofía.

He dragged the scouts one at a time beyond the *pirules*, where they had lain in ambush for him. He removed their high boots, with their thigh-length soft uppers and frayed, blue ribbons. The ankle of the first one—the one with the small derringer bullet in his head and no pants—was surprisingly pale. He was likely the descendent of a white child taken by Indian raiders. He removed the man's silver necklace with the Christian cross. He would bury it away from the body.

The other one—the rock thrower—was darker and seemed more a Spanish-Indian mix. Berta had said they weren't real Indians, but Frank knew enough history to know that skin color had nothing to do with whether you were an Apache or not. And what did any of that mean anyway in 1916? They were what he was—men—and he had killed them, and they were dead weight and vulnerable, and he was dragging them through the dirt, their heads stiff enough to furrow the desert floor, their eyes open and filling with dust.

He lay rocks on them to transfer the sun's heat faster to make them rot, and then brush to hide them from men, but not from vultures. He left each man his long hunting knife and his boots, tucked in beside him. For the life afterward that might exist for them. He scuffed over the drag marks, swept them with a dried mesquite branch. He carried their gun belts and rifles farther out into the desert and buried them.

He transferred his things from his upper saddlebag, including his canvas hat. Tosca was lying on the lower one, where he had kept his two boxes of ammunition, but he had taken the ammunition with him for the attack and so that was not a problem. His saddle was pinned as well. That was probably good. Even if Villistas or Carrancistas found his horse and saddle, they would stop looking for him, assuming he had already come to a bad end. As for the scouts, who appeared to have abandoned Villa, why come looking for them? Why would anyone want to run that kind of risk?

He settled the two new horses, checked their packs, added some things, took others—anything identifiable—and buried them back in the desert. As an afterthought, he went back to the corpses and considered their knives and high boots with the blue ribbons.

He could not decide what to do. *It was good to honor people you had killed,* he thought. It was bad to leave identification for someone who might want to avenge them. He removed the rocks and brush and cut off their clothes. On the lighter scout, he noticed black marks, like thumb smears, above each eyebrow and just below each eye. He touched one of the marks. It was still oily. His companion carried the same marks. They had painted themselves because they meant to kill him. He piled the rocks back on them and rearranged the brush and added some dead cactus. He buried their boots and clothes and one of their hunting knives in a separate place. They would have to go to the next life without them. He kept one knife.

He took the bridle and saddle off the Appaloosa mare, and cut the girth so it would be useless. He put Tosca's halter and lead rope on the Appaloosa and tied her back to her tree. Then he carried the Appaloosa's saddle and tack across the creek and, at some distance, hid it in a thick clump of mesquite.

All the time he worked, he had watched so he would see Sofía when she woke up. He did not want her to think he had left her. When he reached the creek again, she was squatting in the sunlight near the water with her arms around her knees, trying to get warm. He re-entered the water with his boots on, as he had done the night before, only this time it did not matter what noises they made from being wet. The water had cleared overnight and on the bottom, at calf depth, he saw small black snails that left drag marks on the rippled sand. The sun was warm on his back, and when he reached Sofía it seemed natural to lean over and kiss her on the lips when she looked up at him.

"They used me as bait," she said.

"I know," said Frank, and he helped her stand and held her.

He roped the Appaloosa to the sorrel gelding he would ride. Sofía would ride the black mare she had borrowed from Doña Mariana. He tied his rifle scabbard to the sorrel's saddle and slid home the Winchester. He packed his brass telescope. The last thing he did was take the pale scout's hunting knife, roll up his sleeves, and make a long cut into Tosca's belly and pull out her intestines, so the scavengers would come right away and the vultures soon after. With any luck, there would not be much evidence left by the time someone else came along the stream, or the stink would be so great they would not linger. Then he washed the knife and his hands in the stream. He moved a few steps upstream to cleaner water, and washed his face, then packed the knife and mounted.

They climbed to the west, then turned north, riding in the high country. In the plain below to the right, they saw the black smoke of a train. When they passed a particularly thick patch of mesquite, Frank took out the pale scout's long hunting knife—the one that had not been used to cut off his face—and threw it deep into the brush. When they were a good day or two away, he would tie the Appaloosa off to tree, near a trail, close to a village where people were poor, so that someone could find her and use her.

CHAPTER 29

Bathing and Brigands

For the next few days, they kept to the long slopes between the mountains to the west and the vast Chihuahua plain to the east. They would wait in the shadows of *pirules,* talking quietly, watching for followers. They saw single riders, sometimes small groups, but these always veered off in other directions. Frank regularly swept the countryside with the brass telescope.

He saw lone *campesinos* on their way to their fields, sometimes astride a burro, seated back toward the haunches, switch in hand, a machete looped with a string over one shoulder, legs flopping. Often, by time he saw them, they had stopped and were fixed on the spot as if painted, the burro patient, the man's eyes hidden in the shadow of his straw sombrero, his gaze directed over the distance straight at them. Then he started forward again, but always glanced back, watching, wondering who the riders with pale skin and an extra horse were that passed through his country.

Frank and Sofía stopped in secluded places. They bathed in the pools of streams. They washed their clothes and lay them on rocks to dry. They took turns at lookout, holding the Winchester and the telescope. They watched each other bathe. She turned her back to him when she washed. He always faced her when he bathed. She had her derringer still.

She held his rifle, sitting higher up, thirty feet away, watching him, watching the countryside for movement, glancing back at him for long moments. He watched for signs of her smoking. She watched him for signs of mercury poisoning. They admired each other's body. At night, under the stars, they slept spooned together, with their clothes on, chaste, wrapped in blankets and varying degrees of trust. Too much had happened to make love. She held his hand over her breast.

His various kinds of headaches dissipated. His thoughts came more easily. At night, next to Sofía, he considered the question of his responsibility for killing the two scouts. He understood that none of it would have happened if he had not worked in the mine his father managed in Mogollón, if he had not gotten mercury poisoning, if he had stayed out of México.

Sofía had set off a chain of events. Or was it the Apaches who began everything? He concluded that he shared responsibility, not with God, as Mr. Leibniz would have it, but with everyone else. Sofía's husband had been about to shoot a shepherd boy who limped. Sofía had come to claim his body. She had come to his bed in the muddle of her addiction. Maybe she had chosen opium in lieu of confronting a bullying husband. The shepherd boy had chosen to throw rocks at her husband rather than just stand aside and let him take a goat or two. Doña Mariana had chosen to take Frank and Juan Carlos to her house. The Rurales had come to the house with the wounded officer—Sofía's husband. Frank and Juan Carlos had chosen to go with the boys to their swimming hole. The Apache scouts had found them there and Pancho Villa had taken them prisoner.

Then the scouts had fixed on doing what Apaches had done for a long time: steal horses and kill intruders—as well as claim a long-barreled Winchester and a fine brass telescope. They had come after him, and he had managed—as much by luck as cunning—to get the upper hand, keep them from their rifles and their senses. That event had been triggered by Sofía's derringer, though he himself had crossed the countryside with a satchel of cartridges and the intention of putting an end to their pursuit and menace.

He listened to the night sounds and slept in fits and starts. He would accept shared responsibility he thought, but not all of it. This conclusion allowed him to rest. He took it as a good sign that his head did not hurt, and almost never did thereafter.

When it began to gray, he noticed that Sofía's breathing was shallow.

"Are you awake?" she asked.

He nodded, his head moving against hers.

"I'll watch," she said. "You can sleep."

When he woke again, the sun lay across them, and she sat looking at him, the Winchester across her lap. He smiled, glad to see her. She brought the rifle over to him and lay down beside him, toward him, her face close to his.

"You slept for a couple of hours," she said.

As they made their way north, they did little things for each other. Frank carefully moved her extra set of clothes, so they would stay in the sunlight and dry. She heated tortillas on a small *comal,* filled them with bits of cooked goat meat and beans and chiles—bought along the way from women in small houses with tin roofs—and handed them to Frank. They did not talk about the future, though it weighed on them, as happens when people begin to care for each other. But in this case, the present was stronger. They enjoyed each other's company. They laughed at things. They consulted on tactics, how to survive in a country full of various armies, bands of deserting soldiers, common bandits and peasants too hungry to follow the law.

They learned from a farmer that they were nearing El Sueco, the station where Frank had first boarded the train with Doña Mariana and the three vaqueros. They asked other farmers and received the same answer. El Sueco was half a day's walk ahead.

And so, within sight of a small village, near a carefully tended field, with a well-beaten path leading to it, they tied off the Appaloosa in the shade of a *pirul.* It whinnied in protest when they rode away.

Looking back from a different angle, they saw a girl and her mother walking the path toward the cornfield. They would find the horse and begin deciding what to do about ownership. There was no saddle and no bridle, just a beautiful Appaloosa under a *pirul,* next to the field, and what appeared to be two gringos riding away from it. They would be wealthy, because they were gringos, and had no need for another horse.

Sofía waved at them. The girl reached out and took her mother's hand. Neither waved back. They stopped walking and watched Frank and Sofía. They glanced at the Appaloosa tied to the *pirul,* then back at the riders. Frank could see the questions had already begun. The people, now on horseback, who were waving, were friendly. The horse, they would come to believe, was a gift from God. They would use it to plough and carry wood from the mountain. They would never take it to El Sueco, where it might be recognized. For years they would ask where the horse came from, and who were the gringos. And why had God chosen to have them ride by so close, if they weren't going to leave them the Appaloosa they did not need because they were so rich?

Not far down the trail to El Sueco, they rode along an old wagon track that had been worn so deep that the tops of the banks on either side—tangles of trees and bushes—were at about shoulder height. When they came around a turn, they saw two boys, one on either side of the road, perched up on the banks. Frank estimated they were about fifteen years old.

The boys appeared to have been waiting for them. They were too interested. There was no reason for them to be on opposite banks. There wasn't any reason for them to be hanging about. They should have been working somewhere in the fields or nearby mines.

Frank reined in the sorrel gelding. The boys were a hundred feet ahead of them. Sofía waited beside him. Their horses watched the boys' movements. An afternoon breeze stirred in the trees above them, and mottled sunlight fell shimmering across the road. The boys climbed down from their respective banks—each of them dragging an old Mauser rifle behind. Then they stood in the middle of the road, with their rifles held across their chests.

Frank reached down and untied the leather strap that kept the Winchester in its scabbard.

"We could go around," said Sofía, except that the steep banks made that a problem.

Frank did not reply. They sat that way in silence considering the options, listening to the wind in the trees, breathing in the smell of earth and fallen leaves. Reluctance weighed on Frank. He didn't want to detour. He wanted to go forward. He didn't want trouble. He didn't want to show understanding for two hungry-looking children who, by luck or otherwise, might manage to put a bullet through his heart.

"I don't like this," he said. And so they sat there longer, wondering what to do. In the end, Sofía took out her derringer and tucked it under one thigh. Then she unbuttoned the top of her khaki riding dress, withdrew her arms, and folded the top of the dress around her waist. She pulled her white undershirt over her head, and tucked it under the other thigh. Then, bare-breasted, exposed like the figurehead of a ship, she gave her horse some heel, and moved forward. Frank likewise tapped his horse forward into a walk and, at the same time, slid out the Winchester and levered it partially to be sure the first shell was in the breach and ready to fire.

A hundred feet on horseback passes quickly. Frank scanned the banks for other people. There was no one else. The boys took council and then moved to one side of the road. If they had moved to opposite sides, Frank would have raised his rifle. Instead, he kept it in the crook of his left arm. With his right thumb he cocked back the hammer.

Sofía now held the derringer in her right hand, raised, vertical, at the level of her head, but not so her arm blocked a view of her naked breasts.

They rode directly at the boys and stopped in front of them. The boys did not know what to do with their eyes. They held the old Mausers at their sides, butts on the ground. Frank took the Winchester in two hands and raised it a little higher. They were eight feet from the boys. Sofía brought her hand down and propped the derringer, cocked, on the top of her saddle horn, aimed at the boys. They looked back and forth, between her breasts and the ground.

"Where do you boys live?" she asked, her voice cordial.

"Over there," said the taller boy. He did not gesture as to where "there" was. He had a scar that stretched from a cheek to the eyebrow above it. A piece of rope held his pants up. Sofía uncocked the derringer and tucked it under one thigh again. She put on her undershirt, then wriggled back into the top of her riding dress. They boys now spent less time looking at the ground. "What should we do now?" she asked them.

She waited, giving them time to consider the possibilities. They looked at Frank. He had shifted the Winchester so that it was pointing at the chest of the boy with the scar over his eye. The smaller boy had begun to tremble.

"Here's what we can do," said Sofía. "We can go home with you and talk to your mothers. You can tell them what you were doing and what you saw. We can help you tell them." She paused. "Or, you can stick your rifles up on the bank and walk in front of us for a while. We will give you enough money for tacos and *carnitas* in the town." And then, "Is El Sueco far?"

"Not far," said the boy with the scar, at least willing to talk about the deal.

"Or we can put a bullet in each of your heads, cleanly, so there is no pain, and then you won't have to worry about what we tell your mothers."

The boys considered their options for only a short time. They climbed up the closest bank, just high enough to push their Mausers back out of sight from even the most alert eyes.

"Memorize the spot," said Sofía.

The boy who had trembled, but no longer trembled, paced off three long steps toward El Sueco and scuffed a line into the red dirt, from the bank about two feet toward the center of the road. Because the sole of his shoe flapped open, he had to turn his shoe on its side and draw it backward to make the scuff. Then the boys walked ahead of them toward El Sueco. A mile or so down the road, Frank stopped. He fished out a small Carrancista note, printed on cheap paper that had been acceptable currency in Chihuahua. El Sueco might be another matter. He handed it to the boy with the scar, who examined it closely.

"It's a lot," said the boy, looking up at Frank.

"What you were doing was very dangerous," said Sofía. "For everyone."

Both boys nodded. "They didn't have bullets," said the younger boy.

"They didn't even work," said the boy with the scar.

"Very dangerous," said Frank.

The boys nodded and, at the same time, seemed to marvel that the gringo had been able to say something they could understand.

CHAPTER 30

Coins and Kisses

Later, they turned around in their saddles to see what the boys were doing. They had said their goodbyes, but the boys still followed them toward town. The first few times they looked back, the boys had waved. After a while, the distance grew so great that they no longer bothered.

Ahead of them, lower down, they could see El Sueco through the spy glass, which they passed back and forth. American soldiers—presumably part of Pershing's Expeditionary Force—milled about the few buildings that made up the stop. Their horses were assembled at the south end of the station, where Frank assumed they would be loaded. This meant they were waiting for a north-bound train. And that was what Frank was waiting for.

He wasn't sure Sofía waited for the same thing, and for that reason a sadness weighed on him. He thought it possible they would go in different directions, she south and he north. When I used to ask my grandmother about this part of the story, she would say something that was not particularly the truth, "Ask your grandfather—that was before I knew him."

Maybe the story changes, depending on which cousin you talk to. Apparently, they left their horses and tack at the livery stable, a small place overwhelmed by the presence of various armies. All that was left was water. Feed was expected in a day or two.

Campesinos were coming in with burros hidden under loads of dried corn stalks minus the ears – *rastrojo*. Horses didn't like it, but, in small portions, it would keep them alive until they got hay or even better, alfalfa.

They nodded their heads at the stable owner. Yes, the rastrojo would be fine, though neither intended to return for the horses.

Sofía said she would never ride back through the area they had just passed. The conversation had not continued. What they were not saying was beginning to rise like water to the lip of a cup.

They entered the train station. They waited in line in front of the ticket window, an office the size of a closet. Two American officers in line ahead of them were negotiating a price for the four extra cars they had ordered, mostly in impatient English.

"How many people?" the stationmaster asked. He was a small man with runny, nervous eyes.

"One hundred eighty-one," said the main officer, in English.

"*Escríbalo*," said the stationmaster.

"He wants you to write it so he can understand," said Frank.

The officer threw him a look, then obliged and wrote the number down on the slip of paper the master had offered.

"How many horses?"

"The horses are returning overland to their regiment in Casas Grandes," said the officer.

The little man didn't understand.

"*Los caballos regresan por tierra*," said Frank, "*a Casas Grandes*."

The stationmaster nodded. "*Qué tipo de moneda?*" he asked.

The Americans looked blank and turned toward Frank.

"What currency?" Frank said.

"U.S. government vouchers," said the officer.

"*Vales del gobierno estadunidense*," Frank translated.

The little man looked blank. What was their value? No one knew.

*"Cómo se canjean?—*How do we redeem them?"—asked the little man.

Blank looks. "Send them to a bank in El Paso."

Frank translated. The stationmaster shook his head. He said Wilson had an embargo against weapons, ammunition and money.

"Oh goddammit," said the sterner of the two officers. He looked at Frank.

"Cuánto?" Frank asked.

The stationmaster wrote two hundred forty-three. *"Dólares,"* he said.

"I suggest you say all you have is two hundred," said Frank. The officers scowled. Then they nodded.

"Doscientos," said Frank. The stationmaster nodded. The stern officer plucked two Franklin one hundred dollar bills out of a cartridge pouch on his canvas belt and slid them under the window grating.

"Receipt," growled the officer.

"The ticket is your receipt," Frank translated. The officers left without saying thanks or goodbye to anyone. The stationmaster opened an empty drawer in front of him and placed the two Benjamin Franklins in it.

They were about to step forward for their turn at the window when Frank asked, "How close did you come to shooting me with the derringer?"

"Close," she answered. And after a pause. "Twice."

The woman who faced him was a head and a half shorter than he was. He considered her answer. Then he said, "Will you marry me and come to New Mexico with me?"

She had already taken out a small goatskin purse that he had never seen before. She studied him for a moment then stepped forward to the window. She lay a silver one-peso coin on the window sill. It read *"República Mexicana,"* with the image of an eagle, wings spread, holding a snake in its beak. The stationmaster reached out

and turned it over. The other side read *"Ejército del Norte 1915"* –
Army of the North, 1915. A coin minted under Villa's earlier control
of the city of Chihuahua and of its silver mining areas.

The stationmaster nodded. Of all the competing occupation
currencies, silver was the one that spoke. The only question was
how many of these coins would be needed.

Sofía reached out her forefinger and placed it on the coin.
The stationmaster withdrew his hand. You could see she had not
decided how many tickets to buy, nor in which direction.

Frank took a slow deep breath.

Then she said, very simply, "Two for El Paso."

The stationmaster held up a thumb and two fingers on one
hand, and just a thumb on the other. He needed four coins in all.

Frank looked at Sofía. She studied him for a moment. She
took him by the shirt and pulled him away from the window, to
the side, out of the stationmaster's view. There was no one else in
line. There were a few people sitting on benches, including two
soldiers with Springfield rifles held upright between their knees.
They had just come in. Their business seemed to be to watch Sofía
and Frank.

Sofía pulled Frank closer, between herself and the soldiers,
so they could not see her. She reached up, took off his old canvas
hat, pulled his head down, and kissed him on the lips.

It was not a long kiss. It was not a short one either. *"Mi respu-
esta,"* – "That's my answer," – she said.

In another version, also from his notes, she told him she would
shoot him in his sleep with the derringer, if he ever left her. But her
answer came right then, out of sight of the stationmaster and with
the two gringo soldiers staring at them with their sourpuss frowns.

The whole scene seems unfair to my real grandmother, who
routinely referred any questions of this kind to Frank. She had
already died when this particular confidence reached my ears.
Still, it feels like an injustice toward her, recounting this part.

And so I will not dwell on it. Maybe I am still too young to accept that that there can be more than one great love in a person's life.

The stationmaster had waited patiently for the two of them to come back into view. He was grayed and wrinkled. He looked at them through silver-rimmed glasses. At their smiles.

"*Felicidades,*" he said, as they left.

Outside, they approached the American officer who had been ahead of them in line and asked him whether the train would be full. The two armed soldiers had followed them from the station and now came up behind them, holding their Springfields across their chests.

The officer said excuse me, but they could not approach the loading area. Frank did not like the restriction, and the manner of its delivery bothered him. There were certain assumptions in the air, like who owned the trains, the tracks and the right to travel.

"I need to see your papers," said the officer.

Frank had no papers. President Woodrow Wilson had issued an executive order in 1915, in which passports were recommended but not required for persons leaving the U.S. But Frank didn't know that. He did not feel like showing papers, even if he had them. He had a reply in mind, along the lines of, *"I'm sorry, but I didn't catch which part of the Mexican Government you belong to."* But he didn't say that. Sofía squeezed his hand twice, quickly. "What does he mean?"

"He wants to see my papers."

"Do you have papers?"

"No."

"Do I need papers, too?"

"No, we'll walk across the border. I know how."

The officer, now accompanied by the other one, asked who he'd been fighting for.

"No one."

"What are you doing here?"

In the past, he would not have known what to say, but that was no longer the case. "Visiting friends."

"Where?"

"In Chihuahua."

"Where in Chihuahua?"

"The city."

"Chihuahua is controlled by Villa."

"The Carrancistas threw him out."

"What are you doing here?"

None of your business, he didn't say that. "Visiting."

"In a war zone?" The officers took turns, each a detective. They were big men. Frank was just as tall. "Things are quiet most of the time." He tried to be friendly. "Then they erupt."

"How do you know all this?"

"I read the newspaper." Which he didn't.

"Why do you speak Spanish?"

I'm a guest. Just the way you are. He didn't say that either. It was too complicated.

Down the track toward Chihuahua, he saw black smoke. The superior officer, the one who had done the negotiating at the ticket window, said, "You can't board the train."

"We have tickets."

"There's no room, there's a standing order to shoot any irregular forces that approach a U.S. military transport."

This is a Mexican train. Compañía del Ferrocarril Noroeste—The Northwestern Railroad Company—Mexican tickets. Carranza has forbidden Pershing from using Mexican railroads. He didn't say this. I'm not even sure he knew it at the time. "I'm a mining engineer."

"You're carrying a gun, we have permission from Treviño." Which could have been true. Frank had heard Carranza couldn't control his generals.

Frank had the Winchester in its scabbard looped over his shoulder with a leather strap. "We'll ride in the cattle cars."

"Those are U.S. military horses using the cattle cars."

"You're stringing them together and taking them back cross-country . . . not loading them."

Frank's notes show he had a dark moment when he considered using his Winchester to get his way. It was a mad idea, and he dropped it. A moment passed while he briefly reviewed the damage he had already done in the world.

"There's another train coming in the morning," said the officer. Maybe he had turned a little conciliatory. Maybe he had noticed the look in Frank's eyes.

They turned and walked back to the stationmaster. They explained that the Americans wouldn't let them board the train. The stationmaster's eyes flicked around the waiting room, then out the window at the American troops.

"I didn't realize they were allowed to use the railway," said Sofía.

The little man's eyes swept the empty waiting room again, as if spies might have entered, just in the last few seconds.

"They claim to have permission from General Treviño," he said. "How would we know? The lines are down. Everyone cuts them. There are workers looking for the breaks. We'll know more when the next southbound train arrives."

Frank couldn't tell what was worse: a train full of Pershing's men going north or a train full of Carrancistas coming south. The stationmaster was making his calculations. There were Benjamin Franklins to consider, two of them, sitting green in the otherwise empty drawer. Surely it was better to send the Americans up the track and let someone else enforce the railroad ban. The soldiers were all largely sick. Typhoid, influenza, infections—he didn't know which. He could argue a general had given his permission.

The lines were down, how was he to know? After all, they weren't combat troops heading south. And why would the Americans lie? Why would they risk being interred as prisoners of war simply for illegal movements?

"There's a train in the morning," said the little man. "You'll get sick riding with this group. And we don't know what will happen if this train is stopped. American soldiers are on Mexican territory. There are various armed groups that do not worry whether they cause a war between two countries." He paused, looking around the waiting room for possible eavesdroppers.

"Take tomorrow's train. It will be much safer for you. Your tickets are still good," he said, with a kindly face. It was sort of a benediction. So the two travelers left the station.

CHAPTER 31

Rituals

Frank recognized the girl with the basket. She had just changed direction, coming away from the soldiers and toward them. "*¿Camote?*" she asked.

She was still barefoot and poor, her dress worn, but clean, her black Indian hair pulled back in a tail.

Frank wagged his finger to say *no, gracias,* no crystallized sweet potato for him. But Sofía found some coins and asked for two pieces.

The girl set down her basket, took a square of torn gray paper, wrapped two pieces of camote, and handed the package to Sofía.

"*Dos centavos,*" she said.

Sofía gave her a copper *peso.* The girl made the motion of looking for change in the cloth bag hung around her neck. Sofía said she didn't want any change. Pleased, the girl picked up her basket and swung it back and forth in front of her. Sofía went to see if there was a toilet in the station. She handed Frank the package and left. He took a bite of the camote he had not wanted. Then he took another bite. He pointed at the telegraph poles. "The last time I came through here, there were people hanging from those poles."

"You want to rent a corn husk mattress? For the night?" the girl asked.

"You said you could make them whistle by touching their feet."

"The *arroyo* has enough bodies," she said.

Frank didn't understand. He didn't see any *arroyo*. Maybe west, beyond the tracks. He saw green there. He also saw there wasn't much hope for communicating with other places along the rail line. Some of the telegraph poles had been cut down, probably for locomotive fuel. Those that still stood had wires hanging down. One or two still had nooses, clipped through, with thicker areas of tar-like material clinging to the wire.

"The water stinks," she said.

"What's your name?" Frank asked.

"Rosario."

"What water?" Frank asked.

"The *arroyo*," she said. "They pump the water for the trains. Don't stand near the steam coming from the engines. You'll . . . ," and she hung her head over and made a sound like a cat coughing up a hair ball. "We have hot goat's milk, *gorditas* too. Do you want to buy some?"

"We'll think about it," said Frank. "Are there soldiers here?"

Rosario pointed at the Americans near the tracks.

"Others," said Frank.

"They come in trains. None here right now," said Rosario.

"Carrancistas?" Frank asked.

"Soldiers," said Rosario.

Frank nodded. "And the mattresses?"

"My aunt. Behind the stables. And *gorditas*."

Later, Frank and Sofía went to look for the aunt. The train had left, going north with the sick American troops. Half their horses left with the train. The other half waited to be returned the next day in strings toward Casas Grandes. Frank and Sofía found Rosario's aunt. They had blue corn *gorditas* piled with greasy warm goat meat and crumbly cheese, and they drank warm goat's milk from dented tin cups. They sat close to the *comal* and the orange embers under it.

The sun was setting behind the western mountains and the temperature dropped. Even the smell of burning charcoal seemed chilled. Rosario sat on a three-legged milking stool made of mesquite.

"More milk? Another *gordita?*" asked the señora. With one hand, she held her rough brown wool *rebozo* closed in front. With the other, she turned the *gorditas* with her fingers never quite touching the *comal.* When they were through eating, they licked their fingers. The señora gave them pieces of burlap to wipe their hands.

"I washed them this morning," she said.

A little apart, two golden mutts kept a small herd of goats bunched around a pile of cornhusks. Young and old nibbled and raised their heads and watched humans seated around the *comal* with their amber eyes and rectangular black pupils. Behind the fragrance coming from the *comal* hung the smell of the buck's piss on his yellowed front legs.

Sofía chatted with Rosario's aunt. Carrying his satchel and rifle, Frank went to the stable to retrieve the blankets strapped to their saddlebags. Two people were sitting with their backs to the stable wall—probably because it was still warm from the disappeared western sun. They watched him approach with apprehension, he thought, like people who do not belong and who expect orders to move on. But their glances turned to smiles, each instant more certain.

They were a boy and his mother—she dark, with long black hair parted in the middle and straight eyebrows that nearly joined in the middle. She wore a blue and black striped *rebozo* around her shoulders, with one end over the boy's shoulders.

It took Frank a moment. The boy stood up and took one step toward him, with one foot turned in, the leg shorter, so that he wobbled. The mother sat cross-legged in her long, faded magenta dress and dusty *huarache* sandals. With the ease of youth, she rocked forward and stood up without using her arms.

"I know you," said Frank.

"We know you," said the young woman. "You slept in our house."

Frank recalled a more specific image of lying next to her, him stark naked, heavy in his dreams, the sound of horses moving past the hut, the moon shining through the door, inching across the floor, her arms wrapping around him when he returned to the pallet.

"You played the piano, and then you left."

Frank had never heard her speak before. Her voice was pleasant. He remembered stones she had thrown at him.

"How did you get here?" he asked.

"In the mountains, walking, sometimes a wagon passes and gives us rides. A wagon brought us across the flat to here."

They had come, she said, to see the train, for the boy—the limping goatherd, the stone thrower, the defier of armies. They were going to see a doctor about his limp. It caused him pain. The woman seemed very dark compared to Sofía. Very Indian. Very unexpected. Both of them.

"And you?" she asked.

"Heading north," he told them.

"And your horse?" the boy asked him.

"Dead. A terrible accident," said Frank.

They did not ask how. A thing so terrible was private.

"When is the doctor's appointment?"

"Tomorrow."

"Where will you sleep?"

"There's a hay shed next to the señora with the *gorditas*. We were told we could sleep there after it got dark. No one would see."

"You saved my horse and rifle."

She looked at him with brown eyes. The pupils were round, dark and dilated. "A payment for your act," she said.

Frank's eyes started to water. He did not want them to. "I hope you sleep well," he said.

He returned with the blankets to Rosario and her aunt. He hung one of the blankets around Sofía's shoulders. They paid for their supper and two husk mattresses. They said goodnight.

There were empty ammunition crates just outside the hay shed, just at the drip line of the corrugated metal roof. He piled the crates up into stairs. He helped Sofía up onto the roof, steadying her ankles. She took the two mattresses from his hands. He climbed up. They lay on one mattress and pulled the other over on top of them. High in the air, out of sight, hidden, protected from strangers. The stars came out, bright and cold.

He heard the boy and his mother come in and settle in the husk pile below them in the shed.

"We'll have to be quiet," said Sofía.

They undressed each other, without talking. They lay looking up at the stars above them. They listened to the goats—the occasional low drawn-out bleat, the solitary remark by an animal about the night, the dogs that defended them, or the people on the roof.

They made love, her on top, apparently her favorite way. Frank listened for the boy and his mother, just below them. Sofía wanted to say things. He shushed her with a finger to her lips, she sighed and laughed into his ear.

"You aren't armed, are you?" he asked.

"This makes me feel better," she whispered. "It has not been easy."

Frank thought she meant the opium, but he wasn't sure. "You are very sweet," he whispered in her ear.

"You are," she whispered back.

In the morning, Frank and Sofía paid Rosario's *tia* a few *centavos* for well water, a white enameled metal washbasin, two stained but newly washed rags for drying off, and a triangular piece of brown soap with pieces of dried grass stuck to the outside. Sofía went into the reed enclosure first. The señora said she would stand guard and that Sofía could take her time.

Frank splashed his face and drank a cup of warmed goat's milk, from a cup that had a smoky smell to it. Rosario was already out selling camote. He walked toward the station, with his satchel and his rifle slung over his shoulder. It appeared that most of the American horses had already left to return cross-country. There was still a troop of some kind—twenty or more U.S. soldiers and their horses—all of them, horses and men, looking a little sick. Their horses had oozing spots around their mouths and on their hocks that someone had painted with a blue medicine.

He followed a path south, along the tracks, away from the horses. At the vanishing point, down the track toward Chihuahua, he could just make out a black dot. It did not seem to grow larger. He saw no smoke. And so he guessed it was the morning train and that it had run out of fuel, and the crew—maybe the passengers as well—were looking for water or something to burn in the firebox, or both.

He turned around to follow the path back and found himself blocked by a U.S. soldier with a Springfield rifle and an attached bayonet. An officer—a different one from the day before—stood next to the soldier.

"Do you speak English?" asked the officer, in what seemed more a command than a question.

Frank wanted to wash. He wanted more breakfast, and he wanted to see Sofía.

"Good morning," he said.

"You can't board with that," said the officer, indicating the rifle scabbard and the exposed butt of the Winchester slung over Frank's shoulder.

Frank didn't feel like being unpleasant. He made himself smile. "What about him?" He pointed to the soldier.

"You heard what I said," said the officer. He was about Frank's age and had been given the inglorious task of returning the rest of the sick horses and men to the border. The man's eyes were bloodshot. His face was flushed, and he already, on this morning, looked as if he might have a fever. The soldier's hands trembled ever so slightly, as if he, too, were sick.

"This is México," said Frank. "My wife and I have tickets. We're going home. I am a citizen of the United States. I live in New Mexico, in Mogollón, to be precise. This is my rifle." And then he added, partly out of mischief and partly because he thought it might happen, "A regiment of Carrancistas is due here at any moment." As he said this, he pointed at the dark spot on the tracks, still at the vanishing point. "They might be on that train. And I believe you know Carranza has said you may not use Mexican railroads."

This speech gave the young officer pause. He passed a hand over one eye and part of his forehead, as if it were all too much for him.

"I need to know what you are doing here," he asked. At the same time he undid the brass button on the canvas flap that kept his Colt 45 automatic in place.

"Sir," said Frank, having no idea why he used the title of respect in this situation, "I am no threat to you, and what I am doing in México should not be any of your concern."

This he said with a smile and a nod of his head, and he walked past the soldier and officer, who both moved slightly to one side of the path as he went by.

The sun rose higher. The train stayed in the distance. Horses and men coughed and looked miserable at the assembly point. The shepherd boy and his mother returned from the doctor. There was nothing wrong with the boy, she said. All he needed was a raised shoe to ease the limp. They could have it made.

Frank asked the boy to help him. The three of them went to the stable and paid the fee. Frank saddled the horses and led the sorrel gelding and the black mare out into the sunlight.

"I'm sorry about your other horse," said the boy. Frank did not respond.

"You kept these things safe for me once, when other people were after them," he said. "They are yours now." He strapped the Winchester scabbard to his horse, with the rifle in it. "This is to protect your goats," he said. "You still have goats, don't you?"

"Yes," said the boy. "I liked your other horse."

His mother shushed him.

Frank handed the boy the sorrel's reins. "This will be your horse," he said. "He's a little tricky. Sometimes he'll try to peel you off with a low branch. You'll have to think ahead to keep him from getting too close to a tree with low branches."

He handed the reins of the black mare to the boy's mother. He would settle with Doña Mariana eventually. The boy's mother held the reins out away from herself, as if reluctant to believe in her ownership.

The boy carried a once-brown woven wool bag over one shoulder and across his chest.

"Let's put these in there," said Frank, nodding toward the bag.

The boy held it open. Frank fished cartridges out of the bottom of his satchel.

"Be careful. Wherever you shoot, that's where the bullet goes. It can kill someone from a long distance, just like the man who wanted your goats. You remember him? He died from a bullet like these. Make sure there's rising ground behind your shot, so the bullet doesn't continue. Don't try it around here. The horses need care. You know people who can show you."

Frank took their few extra clothes out of their saddlebags and put them in his satchel. He drew the Winchester out of its scabbard. He remembered when his father gave him his first rifle. "Be careful," he said. "Take care of your mother. Tie the horses where you can watch them when you go see about the shoes. Keep the rifle covered with something, so people don't see it. It's loaded, so be careful. The cartridges go in the side, here. The bullet end goes first. When no more go in, it's full. Only put twelve in. So the chamber is empty. That's for safety. Now watch. Lever back. See how the shell comes up? See how the hammer is cocked?"

He showed them how to lower the hammer again with equal pressure between the thumb and the trigger. "Now, lever it again and the shell jumps out." The unspent cartridge plopped down onto the ground and lay half buried in a mixture of dust and pulverized manure. Frank eased the hammer down. The boy bent over, picked up the cartridge and handed it back to Frank. Frank blew it off, tapped it twice on his own head—for luck. It was a little joke—a ritual he had never performed before. He fed the shell back into the magazine. The boy and his mother only smiled a little and did not seem to understand the ritual.

As he spoke, he repeatedly asked them if they understood.

They nodded yes. They understood.

"Remember," Frank said, "do not lever the first shell up into the chamber until you want to shoot. Don't try it around here. Wait until you're away from here."

"You understand?" Frank asked one more time. He was looking at the boy. "Be careful you don't hurt anyone, especially yourselves."

He studied their faces to assess their understanding.

"To find grazing for the horses," he continued, "you will have to ride straight through to the hills and creeks. That's where you'll find the dry weather pastures. Otherwise, you will lose the horses."

"We will ride the horses instead of walk," said the boy. "We know where there is water."

Frank nodded. He looked at the young woman. This was the same woman, but from what seemed like another life.

"Did the boy's father come back?"

She looked at him with her young ancient eyes. He looked more closely to see whether her pupils were rectangular. She stepped forward and kissed him on the cheek. He had to lean over so she could reach him. The corner of her mouth touched the corner of his.

"He did not return," she said. "Thank you for these things. Come back and wash in our creek. It is peaceful and nothing happens. Go with God."

She smelled of wood smoke, goat's milk and chocolate . . . and of oranges. Her bosom was full. There was a nick in her left ear, as if from barbed wire or a flashing knife.

Frank turned and walked away.

32

High Above the World

Time passed slowly. The sun seemed as stuck as the train. Then, just as one was preparing to leave, the other arrived, puffing white smoke from gathered wood. The train then sat in an afternoon heat hot enough to melt it. Frank and Sofía sat under the airy shadow of a *pirul* and held hands. The boy and his mother left on horseback, following the tracks north before they would turn west. A Carrancista officer and five soldiers who had arrived on the train ordered the Americans to assemble their weapons in bags and strap them to the coach roofs where they would not be able to reach them. The Americans complied, too sick to argue.

Two wagons arrived with more wood. Rosario's *tia* sold her reed washing enclosure—to feed to the locomotive—for a two-peso Constitutionalist voucher, which the stationmaster said she could redeem with him. Sofía and Frank moved to the south end of a car with the American troops, who continually coughed and wheezed. The shadows grew longer, the late afternoon turned golden brown. The train jerked forward. The stationmaster, standing just below them, waved goodbye.

The Carrancistas remained behind, looking serious, even doubtful. Others would have to take responsibility for the Americans using the railroad in this time of tension between the two great countries. On the train, white smoke streamed past the top of the window, beside Sofía's head.

She talked about Mexico City and the house she had grown up in. He would like visiting there, she said. They would go there often. He would like her sisters and brothers, and they would like him. They talked with the relief of people who have sailed through a storm and now would have a gentle night ahead of them and the prospect of a helping breeze in the morning. He sat across from her. She leaned forward, put her hand on the back of his neck and whispered in his ear about the previous night under the stars on the roof of the hay shed—how hard it had been to be quiet so the boy and his mother just below them would not hear them.

Her whispers made Frank blush. He glanced around to see if anyone was listening. To hide his embarrassment, he reached forward to move his satchel away, so they could sit closer. Across from each other. Knee to knee.

Something made him bend still farther. He straightened up. The backs of his hands were sprinkled with glass. He looked out the window. At a distance of about two hundred feet, he saw the two horses, the sorrel and the black mare, then the boy on foot, with his arm up defending against his mother's blows, which she rained down on him as she advanced. In his other hand, he held the Winchester, keeping it away from her. As the scene passed from right to left, Frank leaned forward so he could keep them in sight an instant longer. For clarity's sake, he kept them framed in the fist-sized hole in the window.

Sofía leaned back in the corner between the seat and the window and gazed at him with a wry twist of mouth, as if to say, *Close but not close enough. They've got to try harder than that*—calm in spite of what had just happened. An amazing woman. Except that she was not looking quite at him. He reached for her hand. It was relaxed. She was still not looking straight at him.

"It's not funny," he said. And he reached for her jaw and playfully aligned her gaze with his, putting an end to her trickery. The middle finger on his right hand was sticky when he lifted it. There was something wet on the side of her head that he couldn't see.

"Did some glass hit you?" he asked.

His voice was tender and understanding. After all, how could she know, without a mirror?

"Did you feel something?"

The game was beyond funny and had begun to irk him. With a palm on each side of her face, he turned her head. At her temple, he saw what looked like a ripe blackberry that had somehow hit her and now pulsed its dark juice down over her cheek. "Sofía?"

His voice became softer. In his mind, he told us later, he heard a dialogue, but with only him talking. He heard himself ask, as he looked into her face, "For a question to be a question, doesn't there have to be someone listening?"

The young officer who had confronted him so unpleasantly that morning was standing beside him, with his hand resting on Frank's shoulder.

Frank held Sofía's hand. The blood took its time, but inched along the wooden seat, first around Sofía, and then on to Frank, who had moved to be beside her. The soldier who had carried the rifle and bayonet in the morning was on his hands and knees, wiping up the floor with rags.

Frank's right hand held her right hand. His left hand cradled her cheek, with just enough resistance so that her head wouldn't fall toward him. He sat twisted toward her. After a while, the officer took Frank's hand away from Sofía's head and arranged her so that her head rested back in the corner, with her chin on her wet chest.

Maybe because of the expression on Frank's face, the officer said, very gently, "It's not your fault."

Frank wiped his right hand on his pants and stood up stiffly. The officer used his own handkerchief to flick glass off Frank's hands. He handed him a canteen to drink from. Between their coughs and sighs, the two soldiers suggested that it might be a good idea to move the body outside the car where the cold night air would preserve it.

They gave him two U.S. Army blankets. Frank climbed up first. Then they passed Sofía's body up onto the top of the car. Various pieces of baggage were strapped to the roof and covered with military tarps. The officer and soldier helped rearrange the bags, lumpy from the Springfields and cartridge belts inside them, so the body would be cradled and not roll off during the night. They laid Sofía in the opening. Frank slipped off her boots and arranged them at her feet. He brought her legs together. He held her by her ankles, his hands on her black stockings. Then he stepped over a bag of rifles and settled in beside her.

The officer saw what was happening and arranged the blankets around Frank as well. Then he touched him once more on the shoulder. It was a prolonged touch that signaled he cared. Then he nodded and climbed back down the ladder to the passenger area.

A wind blew from the east off the desert. For the most part, it pushed the smoke from the engine away at an angle. It smelled like cactus, *oregano, garambullo, nopal* and *yucca.* Anything from above ground. It smelled like twigs and leaves, like mesquite, creosote and lavender all mixed together—like anything a young boy has ever tried to smoke. It didn't burn hot like coal. For that reason, the train moved slowly. The wind increased, and the breathing was good. It was not quite as cold as the night before.

The cars swayed and snaked as they lined up with each new direction in the rails. The lovers cuddled together, he on his back looking up at the stars, she on her side, tucked in the crook of his arm, with her eyes mostly open, looking across at him with a tenderness he'd begun to grow accustomed to, with the same amused look, her cheeks a little sunken, her skin bridal and luminescent in the starlight.

He thought of Juan Carlos. He thought of Tosca. He thought of Sofía's husband. He thought of the two scouts he had murdered. Then he wept, as he had for Tosca. He wept for all of them. His chest hurt for what he had almost had. His mouth tasted like tin. He could hardly breathe. Faces and events came and went. And from behind it all, a person he could not quite recognize seemed puzzled and asked over and over, *What have I done? What have I done? What have I done?*

He turned his head back toward Sofía. He wanted to see the look again when, at the ticket window, she said she had almost shot him, twice. He caught a glimpse of a boy and girl splashing in the creek at Mogollón. Stay close to the bank.

They waited for the children to sleep. Then they touched each other under the feather quilt and said silly things. There were trips to Chihuahua. He saw *tia* Mariana and *tio* Wu. They were walking to the Chuviscar with Manuelito, the boy stolen from war. The children splashed and played on the same sand bar. He looked down for signs of burnt logs and Juan Carlos' charred bones. On the other side of the river, he saw the beautiful young woman dressed in khaki, striding among the wounded, cutting them, the young ones, from ear to ear.

His breathing grew shallow. He would never return to México. He did not want to return to New Mexico. He wanted the night to last forever. He wanted to feel Sofía's body grow gradually warmer, to have her eyes open from a soft deep sleep at dawn, just as the sun was rising over the mountains to the east and turning the desert pink. Then he would kiss her eyes and keep his lips there while they snuggled, warm in the blankets, high above the troubles of the world.

ACKNOWLEDGEMENTS

My thanks to Maureen and Steve Rosenthal for sharing their stories about the small Mexican town where we all lived; to my writing partner Ricardo Chico who sat across from me in the coffee shops; to Dada, Zilch, Antik and Tal once a week for years, while we wrote and then read to each other, and where I wrote the first draft of this novel; to Fred Hills, who praised my story "Mr. Leibniz and the Avocado" (which became the third chapter of this novel), and who enjoined me to send out my writing before I was "fitted for a walker"; to the Guanajuato Reading Group that listened to me read from the novel; to Mark Sander and Erin Ferris, who eased me into the discipline of negotiating meaning with editors and into the mysteries of punctuation; to Dylan and Laura Bennett, who urged me to start a blog and *make a book;* to Markus Bennett and Cecelia Belle who gave me encouragement and title suggestions; to my editor David Bodwell for sharing his knowledge of México, for insisting that I could do better than I already had and for teaching me an important lesson: Don't fight. Rewrite! To Richard Grabman for guiding me to Editorial Wisemaz/ Libros Valor and for his reassurance and humor, to Tony Cohan for his support and for helping me understand what editors mean when they speak and to my partner Dianne who insisted I record my interview with Fred Hills at the 2009 San Miguel Writers' Conference, so that I could not deny afterwards the supportive things he might say about my writing.

—Sterling Bennett
Guanajuato
December 2012